DEAD

A Review
Edited by

No. 28 (Fall 2020)

3   An Up-and-Comer .... Darrell Schweitzer
    Stephen Woodworth, *A Carnival of Chimeras*.

6   *Lovecraft Country*: A Bumpy But Enjoyable Ride. Greg Gbur

9   A Weird Tarot Deck................................. Michael D. Miller
    Richard Gavin, *Grotesquerie*.

18 Legerdemain at The Last............................... The joey Zone
    Ann and Jeff VanderMeer, *The Big Book of Modern Fantasy*.

21 *Dark*'s Gothic Use of Time Travel.......Karen Joan Kohoutek

29 Other Worlds, Other Voices ....Daniel Pietersen
    Melissa Edmundson, ed., *Women's Weird 2. More Strange Stories by Women, 1891–1937*.

33 Ramsey's Rant: The Urge To Splurge........ Ramsey Campbell

37 Sharpening a Dulled Blade: A Conversation with Jason
    Carney, Editor of *Whetstone* .... Alex Houstoun

48 "A Monstrous Rhapsody on Otherness".......... Jerome Winter
    James Goho, *Caitlín R. Kiernan: A Critical Study of Her Dark Fiction*.

53 Ambiguous to a Fault................................Géza A. G. Reilly
    Michael Griffin, *Armageddon House*.

56 A Trade in Futures ....Dan Raskin

61 Starlight in One's Hand................................. The joey Zone
    Leah Bodine Drake, *The Song of The Sun: Collected Writings*.

65 Nodens in the Nutmeg State .... Edward Guimont
    Sam Gafford, *The House of Nodens*.

71 Sandalwood and Jade: The Weird and Fantastic Verse of
    Lin Carter ....Leigh Blackmore

90 June Ruins Everything .... June Pulliam
    Short Reviews of Streaming Horror Film and Television for
        the Covid Era

Spring 2020

99 *Devil's Night* Investigated: An Interview with Curtis M. Lawson .... Géza A. G. Reilly

111 The Light That Never Warms .... Michael D. Miller
The Lighthouse, dir. Robert Eggers.

117 About the Contributors

DEAD RECKONINGS is published by Hippocampus Press, P.O. Box 641, New York, NY 10156 (www.hippocampuspress. com). Copyright © 2020 by Hippocampus Press. Cover art by Jason C. Eckhardt. Cover design by Barbara Briggs Silbert. Hippocampus Press logo by Anastasia Damianakos. Orders and subscriptions should be sent to Hippocampus Press. Contact Alex Houstoun at deadreckoningsjournal@gmail.com for assignments or before submitting a publication for review.

ISSN 1935-6110   ISBN 978-1-61498-317-0

An Up-and-Comer

Darrell Schweitzer

STEPHEN WOODWORTH. *A Carnival of Chimeras.* New York: Hippocampus Press, 2020. 280 pp. $20.00 tpb. ISBN: 978-1-61498-287-6.

I confess that prior to receiving this book I was unaware of this author, which only means that I have been inattentive, because I see from the acknowledgments that he and I have appeared in the same volume three times now (two of the *Black Wings* series and also Joshi's *Nightmare's Realm*). So if this is a belated discovery, it is a pleasant one, because I find Stephen Woodworth to be a thoroughly readable and entertaining writer. If he seems to stop short of greatness at times, well, so do most of us. But even this can be taken as a compliment, because whenever he doesn't quite satisfy, it is because we want more of what he is delivering.

One of the best stories in the volume, "The Hidden Track," does indeed stop a little short of its potential, although it builds interest very well as the cynical protagonist first tries to sell a century-old recording of a "séance" in which the participants perished hideously, then becomes involved with a professor who is obsessed with that former incident. Four-dimensional beings are responsible. Woodworth does a very good job of explaining and (as far as is possible) visualizing what a four-dimensional being would be like. There is a suitably horrific climax, which is, ultimately, just a suitably horrific climax, rather than a revelation of the terror and wonder of a universe in which monstrous beings live unseen all around us. The premise is very similar to Lovecraft's "From Beyond," although with much better development. But he, or at least the viewpoint character, doesn't leap as boldly into multidimensional strangeness as HPL did in, say, "Through the Gates of the Silver Key." The story is by any standards very good, but I think there was a bit more to be teased out of its ending.

There are Lovecraftian elements in some of the other stories, e.g., "Revival," in which a homeless man hoping for a free meal and a place to sleep finds himself involved in a church of nameless unspeakables of a familiar sort. "Voodoo" is set in New Orleans, evokes old gods, and even involves a descendant of John Legrasse, but the explicitly Lovecraftian or Cthulhu Mythos elements are toned down. This is a wise choice. Surely for such a story to work for a modern, jaded audience, the last thing any writer wants to do is parade out long catalogues of Elder Gods and forbidden books, the way August Derleth always did. Such effusions are not horror stories. They are at best wallowings in nostalgia. They make us smile and think of other, better things we have read before, but they create no sense of dread. The test of a good Mythos story is that it must be effective emotionally, as a story, both for people who have a Lovecraftian encyclopedia in their heads and for people who have never even heard of Lovecraft (should any such exist). Story first, in-references a distant second. Woodworth has that right.

He also shows considerable range. Probably the most unusual story is "The Silent Majority," in which Richard Nixon crawls out of his grave at the beginning of a zombie apocalypse and finally proves his worth as a peacemaker, averting the apocalypse with a speech to the undead hordes. "The Olverung" effectively uses a historical setting (the London of Charles II) and tells of a master thief out to steal a magical bird during a royal performance. One sees an affinity to Fritz's Leiber's Gray Mouser or Jack Vance's Cugel the Clever. Woodworth could certainly write sword and sorcery if the market gave him the opportunity. "Mr. Casey is in the House" is about an obsessive slasher-movie fan who gets his just desserts in a movie theatre haunted by the suicide of a serial killer. "The Colorless People" is about a woman who sees auras and her dangerous boyfriend, who may be a kind of aura vampire. "Transubstantiation" blasphemously deals with a Roman soldier made immortal by the blood of Christ, which not only explains the resurrection but leaves our hero with a problem if he is to endure on earth until the death of the sun. The least he can do is hope for company, so he goes around donating blood to blood banks. Another particularly strong story is "Menagerie of the Maladapted," in which a trafficker in medical specimens discovers the next stage of human evolution, brought on by global warming and environmental collapse.

Lovecraft Country: A Bumpy But Enjoyable Ride

Greg Gbur

The first season of *Lovecraft Country,* developed by Misha Green, has concluded on HBO Max, providing a collection of solid tales, impressive visual spectacles, and significant departures from the plot of Matt Ruff's 2016 original novel that makes the series an often rough but enjoyable ride.

Like the book, *Lovecraft Country* follows the experiences of Atticus Turner, a young Black army veteran, as he, his family, and his friends become deeply embroiled in the occult machinations of a group called the Order of the Ancient Dawn. Atticus's quest begins when he goes in search of his father in Ardham County, Massachusetts (a misspelling of "Arkham"), but the cult and its intrigue have a connection to the Turner family, and it follows Atticus home. Eventually, the supernatural will touch everyone in the family, from Atticus's father Montrose to his Aunt Hippolyta and Uncle George, his friend Letitia, and her sister Ruby. At some points they find themselves allied with members of the Order, and at other points opposed; in the end, however, they must make a desperate gamble to free themselves once and for all from their threat and influence.

Set in the Jim Crow era of the 1950s, *Lovecraft Country* is as much about the real-life horrors of racism and institutional oppression as it is about the horrors of the supernatural. It can be viewed as part of a movement to grapple with the legacy of H. P. Lovecraft, who was an avowed racist yet produced some of the most influential horror of the twentieth century. Tales like *Lovecraft Country* work to reclaim Lovecraft's cosmic horror and allow generations of people whom Lovecraft would have despised to enjoy the richness of his style of weird tales. Another striking and impressive example of this effort is Victor LaValle's *The Ballad of Black Tom* (2016), which also made the case that the horrors of racism are at least comparable, if not worse, than those of an uncaring cosmos.

The book *Lovecraft Country* is broken into chapters that are connected to the overall plot but also serve as horror vignettes, and the HBO series maintains that model. The first two episodes, centered in Ardham County, match the first chapter of the book, also titled "Lovecraft Country," and follow Atticus's first run-in with the Braithwhite family, power players in the Order of the Ancient Dawn. From there, it opens into a series of tales that feel like tributes to classic genres of weird fiction: we have a tale of a haunted house, an expedition into a trapped tomb, an episode of pure body horror, time travel, and encounters with a futuristic alien civilization. Though the overall outline of the show matches that of the book, there are significant departures even at the very beginning of the series that make it a very different experience.

One striking change is the use of visual effects and action. Ruff's novel follows a traditional approach to horror, leaving most of the monsters hinted at but rarely seen. In the series, we get a direct view of monstrous shoggoths in the very first episode. One can imagine the thought process for the series producers, who must have been concerned that they would lose a portion of their audience immediately if they did not provide an immediate spectacle. This approach holds throughout the series. The vignettes in Ruff's novel are often quiet, and even end anticlimactically (but still excellently), but this approach was clearly not deemed to play well on television.

The book *Lovecraft Country* is, at heart, a story about racism and racial injustice, and that is still the primary focus of the series. The series creators opted to make the show a broader commentary on social injustice of all kinds, however, and it includes subplots involving sexism, anti-LGBT bigotry, and even the horrors of living in an occupied country. These plots are welcome but often feel too rushed, as if the writers had much more that they wanted to do but not enough episodes to finish the job. For example, one character, introduced in episode 4 and arguably one of the most intriguing characters in the series, disappears in that same episode, which felt to me like a wasted opportunity.

The final episode of the series also feels rushed, as if the scriptwriters were not quite sure how they wanted the season to end. (They were also clearly leaving open questions that could be resolved in a season 2.) The story matches the book in its broad strokes—a final confrontation with the Braithwhite family—but the details are very different, and rather confusing. New revelations are stacked upon previous ones without time for their impact to be felt. This is a huge contrast with the novel, which weaves together disparate plot threads into a satisfying conclusion. It is also a striking difference from HBO's other buzz-worthy series, *Watchmen,* which tackles similar issues of racism and its long-term effects on people and society but has pieces that fit together perfectly from beginning to end.

Lovecraft Country as a whole, however, is well written and extremely enjoyable. The actors deliver compelling performances, particularly Jurnee Smollett at Letitia and Jonathan Majors as Atticus. The episodes provide thrilling and polished entertainment that, though a departure from the subtle stories of Matt Ruff's book, is nevertheless a worthwhile experience.

A Weird Tarot Deck

Michael D. Miller

RICHARD GAVIN. *Grotesquerie*. Pickering, ON: Undertow Publications, 2020. 287 pp. $17.99 tpb. ISBN: 978-1-988964-22-5.

When an advance review copy of Richard Gavin's *Grotesquerie* fell into my hands, my anticipation levels ran high, knowing much of Gavin's earlier work, and a Mike Davis cover that imposes a saturated Bosch-like landscape suggesting the grotesque. This collection contains sixteen stories from 2013 to 2019. And now the question: Does it live up to its suggestive title?

First, a little background on Richard Gavin. S. T. Joshi titled his short essay on Gavin "The Nature of Horror" in his *21st-Century Horror* (2018), and that title is mostly true to this collection as the stories aim to get into what the nature of horror is, while also often veiled in "folk-horror" etude to the natural world. Joshi's overall characterization of Gavin is accurate: "Richard Gavin (b. 1974) has been quietly amassing an enviable reputation as an author of weird tales that fuse sensitivity to the strangeness inherent in the landscape with a keen insight into human emotions, expressed in prose that provides its own sensuous pleasures all apart from the subject matter." There is also another element associated with Gavin pertaining to the occult. Many stories often include a convincing transmission of occult truth often as shocking as the culmination to an Ari Aster film. For a little more on this, Gavin himself has remarked:

> It has long been a belief of mine that horror is a direct link to the primordial consciousness. I am of the opinion that certain strands of the macabre tale, when wellcrafted, can pry open doorways in the psyche that would have otherwise remained sealed, thus prohibiting a vast panorama of profound personal experience. In order to facilitate this "prying open" process, I

attempt to write fiction that is as close to its transcendental (or perhaps infernal) source as possible.

This has not always been successful in the entire catalogue of Gavin's work, but let us move ahead and pry open the contents of *Grotesquerie*.

"Banishments" leads the collection with an opening storm propelled with elemental prose and figurative descriptions of nature, in this case a powerful storm surge, overcast with dark color and an assault on the senses, not too far from the opening atmosphere of Kurosawa's *Rashomon*. In the surge as two brothers watch a deluge of objects race by in the encompassing flood waters, they find a strange casket among the debris. This object is taken back to the brother's home where it serves as a catalyst to unleash past events about the brothers, Dylan in particular, who we learn has lured his brother, Will, there on false pretenses. None of this is lost on Will: "He envisioned the two of them now as being Pharaoh's daughters, rescuing a floating ark from its reedy doom." The casket is soon discovered to be a curse, and in the tradition of "don't mess with the unknown" our two siblings do not fare well in the events that follow. More importantly, as the opener of the collection, is this story living up to or emblematic of "grotesquerie"? Not so much. If anything, this is "sibling horror," a weird lullaby, pitting brother against brother, in a subgenre awakening readers to the horrors of hereditary bondage and familial belonging.

"Fragile Masks" follows and is not much of a game changer. The opening story, or surely the second story, must speak for the volume, and this one is shy of grotesquerie as well. Set in a remote bed-and-breakfast on Halloween night, it tells of two married couples, Jon and Paige, and Teddy and Alicia; Paige and Teddy were once married, and the story spends its time on the impact of jealousy while we forget about much of the setting and any horror elements, until the end, where we learn Paige has set them up for an encounter with a horrific entity. When this event happens, Gavin hits the reader hard, for it is remarkably unexpected; but everyone survives the horrors, leaving us with a less than convincing internal monologue from Jon about facing our "true selves." What can be said about *Grotesquerie* thus far is that these stories do not promise anything and have shied away from convention in any sense.

"Neithernor" tells a tale of the artist Vera Elan through her cousin in a first-person narration and is a complete shift in tone and style from our opening tales. We feel as if this is in some nineteenth-century era, and echoes of Poe, James, Chambers, and even Machen abound. Along with this interesting shift in style is the exposure of obscure concepts. The tale introduces us to *pyrography*—the art of decorating wood with burn marks, one of Vera Elan's specialties. The narrator isn't too sure about that, as the basic plot focuses on finding Elan, who has not been seen by her family in some time. The execution is a detective story leading to the discovery of the artist and her disturbing imprisonment. Here's where classic Gavin starts to show: the narrative descriptions become murky and actions take on the strangeness of dream logic. Most rewarding, as humans are worked into the pyrography, the grotesque is finally served to the reader.

"Ash Lake occasionally embodies its name. On November days such as this, when sunbeams can scarcely press through the leaden clouds, the lake roils grey and ghostly, taking on the appearance of shifting dunes of ash, like incinerated remains of one who somehow survived the crematorium." Welcome to "Deep Eden," an ever further departure from what we have seen in Gavin's tarot deck of horror, taken to a future setting of some sort, and the haunted place theme is transported to an abandoned mine with a long past and legacy. We are plunged into the weird like a bang in the teeth with no charge for delivery. Evendale, Ash Lake, Dunford Mine are the place names of this decayed setting, set with the myth of the emerald light and "those below." Our narrator, our first female protagonist, motherless and sister to one Rita, hails from a forgotten town whose entire populace has moved below. Gavin builds an utterly convincing world in this story with its dust-bowl atmosphere, pit-canaries, sporadic mine tremors, and life "under the crust" replete with an alien plant thing (recalling somewhat *The Thing from Another World*), while working in the themes of an abusive mother.

When Gavin's prose is spot-on we read moments like this, from our first-person narrator:

> My memories of this town, pale as they are, paint Evendale as little more than a tangle of poorly paved roads lined with dreary structures . . . The houses and shops have all the air of heaped wreckage, of withered husks that no longer shelter withered things . . . A few of them are boarded up with slabs of cheap wood, like coffins bound for Pauper's Row.

The story is really a clever inversion of Lovecraft's "The Festival," with the narrator returning to her family hidden deep in the mine, subservient to a green botanical horror with an unguessed purpose, until the narrator seeks for ultimate enlightenment of its purpose. Her descent into the deeps of this cavernous Eden is again described with fluidity:

> Down, I go, down, staring numbly at the roughly textured tunnel. I begin to imagine the juts and the pockets as being some strange and tedious grammar in Braille, some record of a world that had existed below ours for unknowable years, their entire secret history spelled out here in angled carbon.

Yet, when we think we know where this is going, we are hit with an anticlimactic and almost unmatching resolution. But the story feels as if it works, because it leaves us with the weirdness of it all, not an answered epiphany or terminal climax. The strength of this story is that it leaves the reader wondering, even thinking, is it an effective or weak narrative?

"The Patter of Tiny Feet" is a return to the modern world and the ubiquitous smartphone (the bane of many stories), and here we go again with this distraction in this story. The cover promised nightmares worthy of Hieronymus Bosch, and it's at the point in the collection where it needs to pay off, lest we fall into the fallacy of "never judge a book by its cover." This is not classic weird, but normal horror, almost "normal goes nuts," but with this story the wait is finally worth it. Short and to the point, back to third-person narrative, Sam, a location scout for the film industry, finds an abandoned dwelling off the road, hopefully destined for the feature he is working on. There is a repeated use of the word escarpment that begins here, as our protagonist searches through the interior. The tale is rife with irony. "His grandfather had advised Sam years ago that there comes a time in every man's life when all he wants to hear is the patter of tiny feet." This bears out an early stated premise of the tale, the point of life (any life) is to procreate. This tale is also an interesting play on Lovecraft's "The Picture in the House" and the "searchers after horror" theme:

> For a cold moment Sam imagined one day teaching his daughter or son the thrill of seeking out the special nooks of the world. For Sam, movies were secondary. Their presentation invariably paled against the sparking wonder of discovering the richly atmospheric settings that often hide out from the rambling parade of progress . . .

Of course, for Sam, we know full well that will never be. He finds some pictures, books including *De Vermis Mysteriis,* and *The Trail of the Many-Footed One,* centipedes in a jar, a body in a closet (now we're talkin'!), and finally a well in the backyard into which Sam is thrust as giant centipede food. The story is all sharp, no pauses.

Then we come to "The Rasping Absence." Finally! Dark matter, cosmicism, and the grotesquerie. (My tastes for sure.) What better setting than a mine? A mine in Newfoundland, Bell Island, where Trent Fenner, the protagonist, and one Dr. Newman find an untainted dark matter particle. Gavin makes note of "Canadians and brass tacks" in this story, and it certainly shows as the disruption of everyday life continues. There is a painstaking effort in this story, and some of the others, to humanize characters with pages of narrative time (backgrounds, jobs, wife, kids, etc.)—but why bother? In this cosmic narrative we won't care about the characters for those reasons. Continuing, Trent takes his family to a beachfront vacation town, to wait out the implications of the dark matter discovery. In a tip of the hat to "The Shadow over Innsmouth," a mouthpiece for most of this story, Old Isaac, appears on the beach one day, digging and filling holes, intimating that there is some being tearing through, and Isaac alone must keep the vigilant task of preventing this force from breaking through. It isn't long before Trent becomes obsessed with Isaac and his chore, with dire consequences for himself and his family. There are some brilliant passages where Gavin conveys this:

> But the night was lodged in his head. Constellations shimmered and blinked. They were smeared across the seemingly endless curve of his calvaria, like his very own planetarium . . . He was being drawn into black gaps. Trent felt himself being pulled like a hooked fish into that abyss where even the flesh is forbidden.

Very quickly Trent learns that it is dark matter Isaac is trying to stop, but only too late. In a flip of Matt Cardin, the story asks, what is the cost of the universe's indifference, not from a philosophical view but instead, from one of human loss.

"Scold's Bridle: A Cruelty" is a perfect sick and perverse Poe-like story of corruption, featuring a horrifying rabbit costume recalling the infamous bunny outfit from *Donnie Darko*. This is simply a tale of a medieval torture method, the scold's bridle, the rabbit-like torture helmet worn over "the only human feature" of the human body—the face. It is a morality tale like the best of *Creepy Comics:* what you do for money (a craftsman is asked to forge the bridle for a teacher of medieval studies who wants to use it on his wife) can come back to haunt you. "Crawlspace Oracle" is an even further penetration into the grotesque (and the abhorrence of all flesh) that is a clear tribute to Ligotti, no introduction or conclusion to the narrative needed.

We are now at the halfway mark and, while there is some filler to this collection, the standout stories alone make *Grotesquerie* a worthy volume. "After the Final" concludes the Ligottian sentiment of the prior tale with a frightful humorous brief search for the one and only macabrist Professor Nobody (alluded to in Ligotti's *The Conspiracy against the Human Race*). This reads as a personal note from Gavin to Ligotti saying: "I am one of you." The protagonist of the story, one Maximilian, utters: "And then it all became so obvious. For what were your lectures if not impressions of life beyond the theoretical, echoes of the palpable nightmare that succors us all?" That alienation leads Max to invent a special white powder causing "Normals to wither inside their pathetic little houses, crumpling like puppets with clipped strings." Max is soon commanding a plague-ship more sinister and disease-ridden than Matt Cardin's Sick-Seeker cult. Yet even these events leave the narrator wanting and alone asking, "Who else might draw equal delight from this endless nightmare of being?"

The remaining stories vary in pace and purpose. "The Sullied Pane" is a story of family horror about the curiosity of the family of one's spouse. A mystery story with a possible moral—be careful what you spit on. The story continues the trend of very balanced, strong female protagonists featured in this collection. "Cast Lots" and "Notes on the Aztec Death Whistle" are the weakest stories in the book, and not much space need be given to discussing them, but "Headsman's Trust: A Murder Ballad" is a real gem. If Ingmar Bergman were to have attempted a Gavin story, this would be it. Here the creep of folk-horror is prominent as our female protagonist is drafted into the service of a headsman in a medieval setting, moving from town to town and collecting heads and burying corpses, only to discover the headsman's secret ritual of keeping his victims' souls, letting them fly from the empty husks in the shape of a great bird, and soaring off to new lives. Our protagonist then learns her time has come as well, and is replaced by a young disciple, as the headsman sends her off to join the other souls "free from the tyranny of the head."

The last three stories form a sort of trifecta echoing all the principles in Gavin's remarks quoted in the opening of this review, as close to the source of the horror as possible; in this case, a folk-horror Gavin-style milieu. "Chain of Empathy" is a witchcraft tale straight out of Haxan: the style is old-world classic, the past long gone yet we feel it, Gavin making it new. Our protagonist is Berthe, a witch in training, using a blacksmith's nail found embedded in a tree trunk to communicate with her master.

> Berthe had been happy to allow her superficial self to steer her. Life was much steadier this way; the lulling pattern of chores and family and rest and church on Sundays. But her la-

tent self was forever giving hints of itself, teasing her with not only its grand scope but also how inextricably bound to her it was. Berthe could feel it stirring to the base of her spine, and the back of her skull; an iceberg showing glimpses of its drowned base when the waters are tossed. Its influence upon her had become so strong that in her private diary Berthe had begun to refer to this second self as "the master."

Gavin throws the reader right into Berthe's story, no explanation. We learn bits of lore along the way: hearth-eaters, the marlinspike (blacksmith's nail), and grave hands. All in all, a beautiful story of alienation and suicide. Gavin weaves a narrative spell complete with verbal, somatic, and material components. "Three Knocks on a Buried Door" is a modern twist on the same theme, only this time knocking on doors replaces actual witchcraft. Kolkamitza's recently deceased girlfriend, a witch of some note, dies before she is able to complete the last knock in her quest to visit for random haunted places. With a little investigative work, Kolkamitza finds the location of the last haunt and gives the required three knocks, opening the door to a hidden room buried in the backyard. This of course, is a trap set by Kolkamitza's deceased wife, in order to trap him and use his body as bait to free her and dozens of other souls trapped therein. This story more than any other carries out the Gavin sentiment of "prying open doorways into the psyche that should have remained sealed."

"Ten of Swords: Ruin" revisits again the idea of horror seeking to destroy families. Here we have two sisters, Celeste and Desdemona, who know little about their parents, and even less about their mother. The story concerns the sisters finding their mother's deck of tarot cards and hiding one of the cards from the deck in the family crypt. This event unleashes a series of portents about their family, revealed secretly, card by card, until the mother, possessed by an unknown entity, seeks to reclaim the cards, and in short order she murders her husband and then attempts to kill her daughters. The cards are used again, at first to elude her mother, moving off their ancestral island through the card of the chariot; but also this act separates the two sisters. Even stranger, the cards now seem to possess the sisters as they had their mother, and they each find themselves alone in the worlds of the tarot, with one of them, Desdemona clinging "to the hope of reunion." Like most stories in *Grotesquerie,* "Ten of Swords" sets up its own world, immerses us into the lives of the characters, then goes off into directions unpredictable and ending often allusively and unsettlingly, with the reader wanting more; yet, in some strange way, it satisfies with bewilderment.

Grotesquerie is not a perfect collection; it contains a few too many stories, some of them not well balanced with the others. However, the success of the remarkable stories far outweighs the lesser. *Grotesquerie* is like a tarot deck, with major and minor arcana. And the book itself is one of the major cards in Richard Gavin's deck of weird things.

Legerdemain at the Last

The joey Zone

ANN and JEFF VANDERMEER, *The Big Book of Modern Fantasy*. New York: Vintage Books, 2020. 876 pp. $25.00 tpb. ISBN: 978-0-525-56386-0.

"The Ultimate Collection" presented here is "the last anthology together" from the VanderMeers. Supposedly.* Ninety-one stories include not only "A Mexican Fairy Tale" (1988) by Leonora Carrington but the gossamer-winged surreality of Carrington's "Myth of 1,000 Eyes" (1950) scampering across the front wraps. For giving Carrington's distinctive *visual* voice current mass-market exposure, the editors should be commended alone.

In *The Big Book of Classic Fantasy* (2019) and earlier anthologies such as *The Weird* (2011) the VanderMeers "tried to be objective about classic authors . . . for example, Robert E. Howard" and, heaven forfend, that "problematic" H. P. Lovecraft. For this Big Book, they seem to not be holding their editorial noses as much and are better for it. They are on surer footing among their contemporaries. They are not trying to define examples of "steampunk," "The New Weird," etc. or retrofit older works to support a thesis. There is, however, a reiteration in this book's introduction that "Fantasy becomes something of use to a writer to make a political or social statement. It's not just a mode . . ." that seems to apply a lot less to a fair amount in this collection. There is no "agenda," for example, to Garth Nix's yarn "Beyond the Sea Gate of the Scholar-Pirates of Sarsköe" (2008) featuring the swashbuckling Sir Hereward and his superior, Mr. Fitz, a three-and-a-half-foot-tall sorcerer—who also happens to be an animated

---

*The editors mention in the introduction (and in recent interviews) the idea to assemble an anthology of Latin American women fantasy writers. Given some pleasures provided in this Big Book, may bright doubts be cast on resolutions otherwise.

puppet with a painted face on a papier-mâché head the size of a pumpkin. No agenda save fun.

Three writers appeared previously in this volume's *Classic Fantasy* companion. Two other stories (by Margaret St. Clair and Elizabeth Hand) were already in *The Weird*. However, selections by J. G. Ballard, Paul Bowles, and Gabriel García Márquez are finally offered here due to the clearance of publication rights.

The Márquez tale of "A Very Old Man with Enormous Wings" is a perfect example of what some might call Magic Realism, with an overabundance of magic pleasing this reader. Written in 1955, it is contemporary with similar work stateside by Ray Bradbury—especially his collection *The October Country,* which was also published in 1955—who is inexplicably not represented in this collection despite a mention in the introduction to the Greg Bear story in this volume. According to an *Entertainment Weekly* interview with the VanderMeers, Stephen King "really wanted to be in this anthology." And is—it is a shame Bradbury is still not around to lobby for himself.

In that same May 4 interview, Anne VanderMeer speaks of "this huge world of influence, back and forth" among fantasy writers. Jack Vance's "Liane The Wayfarer" (1950) included here is a mordant travelogue through the Dying Earth, that series long acknowledged as a worthy successor to Clark Ashton Smith's tales of Zothique. M. John Harrison's "The Luck in the Head" (1984) is a tale of Viriconium following that. And Jeff VanderMeer's own tales of Ambergris—a new edition to be published December 2020—rest on *those* foundations. (Far from *sui generis,* VanderMeer's *Borne* [2017] has an ursine ancestor in Richard Adams's *Shardik* [1974]—a writer also surprisingly absent in this book.) Ann was an editor for *Weird Tales* from 2007 to 2011. She includes writers from that tenure: Rochita Loenen-Ruiz, Ramsey Shehadeh, and Erik Amundsen, the last whose "Bufo Rex" (2007) is a carbuncle of poisonous black humor.

Fred Chappell's "Linnaeus Forgets" (1977) is A Day in the Life of Carolus Linnaeus spent in his greenhouse, while "Alice in Prague *or* The Curious Room" (1990) by Angela Carter is—well, you should just read everything by this woman—

dedicated to Jan Švankmajer and his film *Alice* (1988) but stars John Dee and his assistant: not Ed Kelley, but Ned Kelly the highwayman. "What is the use of books without pictures?" Dodgson's Dreamchild would ask. Tove Jannson's "Last Dragon in the World" (1962) has text *and* Jannson's illustrations from this Tale of Moominvalley. The introduction to this Big Book mentions "a preponderance of dragons." This is the only one you'll ever need. Utterly charming.

"The Fey" is depicted from both sides of The Fields We Know: Sylvia Townsend Warner's "Winged Creatures" (1974) and Caitlín R. Kiernan's "La Peau Verte" 2005). Victor LaValle fights a troll! Well, in his modern folktale "I Left My Heart in Skaftafell" (2004) he does, while Maurice Richardson's Engelbrecht goes "Ten Rounds with Grandfather Clock" (1946). Crazy stuff, but it all works.

These are all just highlights, but I must list at least one more. Rosario Ferré's "The Youngest Doll" (1972) could have fit the editors' criteria for *The Weird*. Women's rights and income inequality *are* factors in this story, but it is foremost definitely one of the creepiest stories, you, *Dead Reckonings* reader, will ever come across. After all the anthologies Ann and Jeff VanderMeer have done, there are still stories we will be lucky (?) to get behind our eyelids. The legerdemain of this last collection being The Charm.

Dark's Gothic Use of Time Travel

Karen Joan Kohoutek

It would be easy to hear the premise of the German Netflix drama *Dark* (2017–20) and envision a European knock-off of *Stranger Things*. It begins with a boy going missing in the woods outside a small town, one that's home to a mysteriously looming industrial compound (in Hawkins, Indiana, this is a Department of Energy front for reality-bending Cold War physics experiments; in the German Winden, it's a soon-to-be decommissioned nuclear power plant). Both are set, entirely or partly, in the 1980s, using '80s pop songs for effect, along with moody, evocative synthesizer scores.

Given all that, it's surprising how radically different, in tone and theme, the two turn out to be. While *Stranger Things* has its share of eeriness and horrific imagery, it blends in enough humor and open nostalgia to create an ultimately optimistic impression. *Dark,* by contrast, has a humanistic quality, empathetic toward the struggles of its flawed characters, but the tone is much, well, darker, visually and thematically.

The plot of *Dark* hinges on time travel, the far-reaching implications of time paradoxes, and eventually alternate dimensions. A twisted, intricate web of connectivity develops among a set of families, playing out over multiple time periods. In doing so, it explores themes of causality, regret, and the idea that if "everything is connected" is true, it's not necessarily always good, and certainly not always comforting. It recognizes the Gothic potential of time travel, using its reality within the story, and the implications of paradox, to Gothic effect.

German art and philosophy have the popular connotation of a dark and heavy tone, which the show leans into. In the Gothic's early days it was often identified with Germany, as was the related literary genre of Romanticism, with leading figures such as Samuel Taylor Coleridge who were strongly influenced by German philosophers and writers. Gothic potboilers were often described as *schauerromans,* or "shudder-novels"; concepts like the "poltergeist" and the "uncanny" (from the *"unheimlich"*) would be brought into English from German ghost stories.

The earliest wave of the Gothic began in 1764 with the publication of Horace Walpole's *The Castle of Otranto* and found huge popularity with Ann Radcliffe's *The Mysteries of Udolpho* (1794). In the satirical *Northanger Abbey* (1817), Jane Austen names seven contemporary novels as representatives of the genre. Of them, five are either translations from the German (*The Necromancer* and *Horrid Mysteries*) or subtitled as "A German Story" or "German Tale" (*The Castle of Wolfenbach, The Mysterious Warning,* and *The Midnight Bell*).

The word "Gothic" has grown far removed from its original connection with Germanic barbarians and its later association with church architecture. It has developed a popular meaning related to the earliest literary manifestations that originally brought the term into the popular consciousness as a literary genre, but tending to emphasize different elements. When something is described as "Gothic" today, it often refers to a certain flavor, more eerie and melancholy than overtly horrific, and frequently rooted in old-fashioned imagery that short-hands an atmosphere of dread. Some of the elements share similarities with the older fiction: crumbling mansions, graveyards, sinister natural settings, and a somber tone that reflects an awareness of mortality, if sometimes with a dash of camp. A ghostly woman in a long gown is more Gothic than a hulking man with a knife; a quiet but cobweb-strewn castle is more Gothic than a suburban murder scene.

While this general conception of the Gothic endures, many of the themes and tropes from the literary Gothic's formative periods have largely disappeared from popular use, but do play important roles in *Dark*.

Castles and ruins certainly appeared as prominent settings for Gothic fiction, and this imagery has continued into the present, thanks to the popularity of the novels *Dracula* and *Frankenstein,* along with their adaptation into the Universal monster movies. The once common use of the natural world as enticing but threatening, and elemental dangers like storms and floods, are much less prevalent in contemporary works.

The "dark and stormy night" has become a joke in such disparate works as James Whale's 1932 film *The Old Dark House,* the *Peanuts* cartoon, and *The Rocky Horror Picture Show* (1975): probably a result of modern technology and transportation making nature much less of a common threat.

The natural world, though, particularly forests and caves, was as key to creating an identifiably Gothic atmosphere as were the crumbling castles, and *Dark* fully indulges in imagery highlighting the threatening nature of forests and caves. Its town is nestled in a huge, deep forest, and the cinematography continually highlights this as an intimidating natural setting, visually dwarfing the human figures and settings within it. The system of caves outside of town is central to the story, and its dark, sinister opening provides the show's most often-used image, seen in its advertising and on the covers of its soundtrack CDs. The cave has its own unnerving theme music, rendering every approach to it uncanny.

The early cycle of the Gothic depicted the forest as not only atmospheric on its own, but containing a frequently used trope: criminal conspiracies (from simple thievery to kidnapping and murder) that were hidden in these natural settings. The ever-present Italian *banditti* of Ann Radcliffe's influential eighteenth-century novels are a well-known example, but there are many forms of this threat, from bands of highwaymen to secret groups of Templars and Illuminati.

In line with this, *Dark* features a generations-spanning group of conspirators, a secret lodge, which possess knowledge hidden from the general population, even as their lives are intimately affected by events they know nothing about. Their activities include kidnapping and murder, rendered almost fairytale-like, as they pluck children from the woods and caves.

The most significant link between *Dark* and the early Gothic is the once very common, almost obligatory, trope of lost-and-found families and mistaken identity, often leading to accidental incest (sometimes, luckily, a near-miss). The incest taboo occasionally appears in more contemporary films with a Gothic tinge, but not with the "long-lost relative" twist. There are more examples of this convention than can be given here:

characters with unknown or mistaken identities, dramatically revealed by a complicated backstory, and usually, but not always, before it's too late to prevent an incestuous union, abound in nineteenth-century Gothic.

Just a few examples: in the 1807 story "The Cave of St. Sidwell," an abandoned foundling is rescued and raised by a hermit, himself a disguised nobleman, who pressures her to marry him once she's grown up. By dramatic chance, she's revealed to be his long-lost daughter, and the handsome young stranger she really loves turns out to be her cousin, whom she marries in the happy ending. *The Mystic Sepulchre* (1806), a fairly blatant recycling of popular plot elements, contains a whole slew of characters who aren't what they seem and don't know who they are, culminating with the discovery that, through a complicated set of machinations, the young heroine has married her brother. The further revelation that she was switched with another girl as a child gives her, as an adult, a new name and identity in the eyes of the world, which might normally be a shock to her sense of self, but comes as a welcome rescue from incestuous love. Even Horace Walpole, the founding father of the Gothic, whose other work was often fairly light in tone, plays the horror of accidental incest absolutely straight in the drama *The Mysterious Mother* (1768).

For people in a world full of stratified social hierarchies, with little opportunity for movement between the classes, this could be a wish-fulfillment narrative, a gender-neutral Cinderella story. Any peasant with notable physical attractiveness, or a perceived nobility of manner, might turn out to be the lost son or daughter of the upper classes, ready for elevation to wealth or status. The shadow side of this fantasy reflects a negative potential side to not knowing who you are, in a corresponding uncertainty of identity. The potential for accidental incest plays out these fears in a dramatic form.

This theme doesn't seem to resonate much with modern audiences. Child abductions, switched or abandoned infants, and runaway spouses, those staples of Gothic plotting, still turn up in soap operas, sometimes even leading to the threat of incest, but these plots have become detached from an association with the Gothic. They no longer have the frisson to appear among the genre's standard imagery.

In *Dark,* the use of time travel allows for similar displacements, with multiple characters taken out of their "natural" places, so they are not known or recognized. In some cases, their true identities are known to themselves, but concealed from others for different reasons (like Michael, who became trapped in the past as a boy, or Claudia, who travels back to tell her youthful father she's sorry for something that will happen when he's an old man). The identities of other characters, though, are a mystery to themselves and everyone in their lives (like Charlotte, abducted from her parents and hidden in the past as an infant).

Most prominently affected is the central couple, teenage Jonas and Martha, whose tentative romance began before either had any idea of the complicated family histories that led to their births. In a traditional Gothic, this would be the result of more clear-cut human villainy or accidents of fate, but here they are caught in a series of ever more complicated time paradoxes.

In the year 2019, Martha's younger brother Mikkel went back in time to 1986, grew up, and fathered Jonas, so unknown to either of them, their romance is between aunt and nephew. Martha's other relationship, with Jonas's best friend Bartosz, is also tangled, since Bartosz would also later end up in the past, becoming the father of Agnes, the grandmother of Ulrich, who is Martha and Mikkel's father. Even more complicated: Signe, the wife of Bartosz and mother of Agnes, is Jonas's future half-sister, who has also became displaced in time.

In the foreground reality, seen before any of these complications, or the reality of time travel, has been revealed, Martha's father, Ulrich, and Jonas's mother, Hannah, had an affair. Neither of them ever learn that Hannah, Signe's mother, is his great-grandmother. Nor do Ulrich and his lifelong nemesis, the policeman Egon, ever learn of their relationship, that Ulrich is his direct descendant.

The more the show reveals the connectedness of the characters' lives, the more family relationships and personal identity are rendered increasingly mysterious and unknowable, even uncanny. Reality is disrupted, and the most solid foundations of identity are suddenly unreliable, a shifting sand. The characters move from the seeming dull ordinariness of their lives into the repercussions of time paradoxes and time loops. In a rich field of metaphor, they don't know who they are, and they don't know who the people in their lives are, and they don't know how to relate to one another. This has seemingly small, realistic consequences; for example, Jonas's father Michael loves his family, but his displacement and subsequent alienation lead to a depression that shadows their lives. There also terrible, tragic consequences, as children kill their parents, parents kill their children, and lovers betray each other.

The existence of time travel, and a bridge to an alternate dimension, rooted in modern physics, creates a destabilizing effect similar to the uncanny elements of early Gothic novels, even though the latter are based on a more openly metaphysical sense of evil, sometimes human and sometimes supernatural.

While there is no evidence that *Dark* purposely references common plot points from the early cycle of German-themed and German-inspired Gothic writing, the connection provides an evocative echo. What's significant is that, despite the passing of time and so many changes in the world, the underlying themes still resonate. The specifics of how they come into play have changed immensely, but the underlying human concerns are much the same.

These narratives put into question all the external sources of identity, the ways it is defined by external relationships and definitions—wife or daughter, hero or criminal—and how those external sources affect the internal sense of self. Unknown connections between the characters unravel the relationships between them, finding its clearest symbol in accidental incest, which turns a bond of love and understanding into one of horror and separation.

The rendering of personal identity into something mysterious and unknowable complicates the channels of causality: while these always exist, the presence of time travel draws attention to them. Someone traveling from 3020 to 2020 might be concerned about stepping on a butterfly and changing the future, but the people living their present in 2020 don't worry about stepping on that butterfly at all. They aren't concerned about the unknown effects their minute actions will lead to in the future, even if those effects might be catastrophic.

In the traditional Gothic, and even in more contemporary versions, we see the long reach of events that may have been forgotten, but the effects continue to influence the present. Familial curses and ghosts from the bygone past provide metaphors for the way we lose our knowledge of the past, even while it is, in a way, still present. A time-travel narrative allows for the exploration of this causality, something that, as we travel in one direction through time, we are able to gloss over and ignore. Cause and effect are lost in the flow and complications of life, but when the linear flow of time is disrupted, causality becomes more visible.

Not only does the past influence the present, but the present influences the past. With time travel, this can be a literal fact in the storyline, while representing a common human experience, by which later knowledge can color our memories or allow us to understand past events more deeply. This is especially true when it comes to human character: a part of the child still exists within the adult, and the seed of the adult already exists, at least in potential form, within the child.

As time travel explores causality, it can also be a vehicle for regret, to play out the feeling that "if only I could do it over, I'd do things differently," whether that might have been possible, or whether the question contains an element of fatality, suggesting that it couldn't have happened differently.

The clearest example of this theme in *Dark* occurs when young Mikkel is first thrust back in time to the 1980s. In 2019, his parents are ragged with grief, desperate to find their missing son. But in 1986, when they're teenagers, he goes to them for help, and they make fun of him. They don't know what they've done, or that in helping a stranger, showing him kindness, they would have directly helped someone they love most in the world. It's a punishment without judgment: just a tangle of causality.

This creates a much more somber tone than the superficially similar storyline in *Stranger Things*. There, the mother triumphs in her overriding will to find and save her child.

Mikkel, though, is eventually found, but he can't be brought back, and while he lives a life that isn't entirely bleak, it ends with his suicide. All this makes *Dark* more "Gothic," in the popular sense.

The series reinforces the importance of causality with more linear examples that don't rely on time travel. Out of anger, a jealous teen falsely accuses the boy she loves of raping another girl, and this action fuses him and her rival, who was previously ambivalent about commitment, closer together, so they eventually marry. Then, if this same couple hadn't once played a cruel prank on a classmate, his brother wouldn't have walked her home to allay her fears, and he wouldn't have been in the place where he was abducted, a loss that would devastate his family.

Causality is entwined with the personal, since human personalities and motivations influence events as much as larger impersonal forces. *Dark* raises the difficulty of tracing the origins of things. Is a car accident caused by the storm that impairs driving conditions, or by the argument that led the driver to head out on the road at a particular time? One person's mistake, or temptation to act in a particular way, has ripples of consequence through time and across the lives of uncountable strangers, and influences those they love in unforeseeable ways.

As it deals with the past, *Dark* is perhaps more powerful for not directly referencing the legacy of Nazism. Of the numerous time periods visited, past and future, no time period is visited with any connection to the war or Hitler's rise to power, and no historical trauma these events have imprinted on the village or its people are mentioned. Doing so would risk overwhelming the story, tipping it away from what it's saying about the human condition throughout all times, not as a tragedy that happened in the past and has now been moved beyond. The past it reaches to is much farther, more formative than that, and the chain of events, leading to other events, shows "how little we understand of the world."

Other Worlds, Other Voices

Daniel Pietersen

MELISSA EDMUNDSON, ed. *Women's Weird 2: More Strange Stories by Women, 1891–1937*. Bath, UK: Handheld Press, 2020. 195 pp. £12.99 tpb. ISBN: 978-1-912766-44-4.

I very much enjoyed the first *Women's Weird* anthology (you can read my review in *Dead Reckonings* 27), so I was excited to see the announcement of a second volume in the series, once again edited by Melissa Edmundson. In the introduction to that initial book, Edmundson said that the stories she wished to "showcase a wide variety of themes and represent the various ways women interpret the Weird in their writing." From solidly weird tales of ghostly hauntings and unseen things to more subtle stories of lost children and malevolent housekeeping, *Women's Weird* contained a vast range of subjects reflected through the lens of female experience. In *Women's Weird 2* this concept is maintained but broadened by not only "expanding into new territories" in a geographical sense—this second volume includes work set in Australasia, India, and South America as well as the UK and US—but also by seeking to "hopefully challenge the already blurred boundaries between the Weird, the Gothic and the ghostly," Thankfully, that "hopefully" is a touch of modesty and Edmundson has more than achieved her goal by presenting us with another wonderful set of near-forgotten stories.

Yet if these stories are near-forgotten, then it might be surprising that a number of the authors are not. One of my favorite pieces in the anthology is "The House Party at Smoky Island," written by none other than Lucy Maud Montgomery, perhaps more famous as the creator of the *Anne of Green Gables* series. Published in *Weird Tales* for August 1935—alongside Clark Ashton Smith's "The Treader of the Dust," no less—Montgomery introduces us to a cast of characters (Aunt Alma, Judge Warden, Old Nosey, et al,) who wouldn't seem out of place in an episode from the misadventures of Bertie Wooster. Gathered together for what becomes a "flop" of a party, the group spend the "dank, streaming night" bickering and eventually resorting to that old party favorite: telling ghost stories. And it is here, almost with a single line, that Montgomery masterfully pivots the story from a fairly flimsy vignette to something that quickly becomes genuinely chilling. The sense of vertigo is palpable; as the narrator himself admits, "I felt sick—very, very sick." Where a less accomplished writer would use this to horrify and repulse the reader, Montgomery allows the unearthly energy she summons to bring harmony and resolution. It's an astonishing piece of writing. In a note written just before her death Montgomery lamented that "I have lost my mind by spells and I do not dare think what I may do in those spells." The ambivalent meaning of "spells" can only make readers of "The House Party at Smoky Island" wonder what else she could have written had she pursued the weird further.

Another standout is Barbara Baynton's "A Dreamer," which, as Edmundson notes in the introduction, is one of the volume's stories that "concern themselves with haunting, even if no ghosts are present." The narrative concerns little more than an unnamed woman hurrying home through the night. She travels from the train station—populated solely by "an ownerless dog, huddled, wet and shivering"—through a building storm until, in the dark, she realizes she has lost her way. Recklessly, she cuts across the Australian bush and, guided toward half-remembered landmarks silhouetted by lightning, she manages to cross the storm-swollen creek between her and her childhood home. The unsettling feel of "A Dreamer" doesn't come from the narrator's peril but from the eerie feeling that the natural world has itself turned against her, perhaps due to the guilt she hesitatingly admits to feeling. This animosity is made explicit: "The wind savagely snapped [the willow branches], and they lashed her unprotected face. Round and round her bare neck they coiled their stripped fingers. Her mother had planted these willows, and she herself had watched them grow. How could they be so hostile to her!" This brings to mind the similar, unearthly animosity of similar, unearthly trees in Blackwood's "The Willows"; and although "A Dreamer" contains no supernatural events, it is redolent with the same terror.

For me, however, the anthology's masterpiece is Katherine Mansfield's "The House." Barely ten pages long, this tells the story of a woman, Marion, who seeks shelter from a violent storm—"no amethyst twilight this, no dropping of a chiffon scarf"—in the porch of an empty house. Here, where the wind is "so cold, to eat into your bones," she rests for a moment, curious memories of this house lingering in her mind, and she drifts off to another place entirely. Unexpectedly, this place is a far remove from the "autumn rain and falling leaves in the hollow darkness" of the storm. She explores the house, now warmed by roaring log fires and populated with a maid and husband she only half recognizes. There is a child somewhere, but she cannot bring herself to think of it fully: "Each time he mentioned the . . . each time she felt he was going to speak of the . . . she had a terrible, suffocating sensation of fear." The story progresses to an inevitable revelation as Marion is called away by a voice she fears but cannot resist.

"The House" is a slight tale, again more of a vignette in many ways, but it has depth behind the obvious narrative. Mansfield herself was bisexual and part of the bohemian circle of the Bloomsbury Group. Her marriage to George Bowden seems to have been largely for the sake of appearances. It's hard not to read "The House," with its ambivalent and cautious attitude to what would have been considered domestic bliss at the time, as Mansfield's own struggle with the inability to live her life as fully as she might wish. Crucially, the story ends with an implicit criticism of materiality and the traditional focus on ownership, whether of possessions or more subtly through marriage: two characters who appear at the end of the narrative are less worried about the eponymous house being haunted for the haunting's own sake than because of the effect it will have on the house's value and desirability on the market. It is no coincidence that Marx describes capital as "vampire-like" with a "thirst for the living blood of labour" when we think of how consumed we can be with our possessions and the means through which we come to possess them.

Whether this is a conjecture too far is arguable, but it's undeniable that Mansfield takes some of the core elements of weird fiction—abandoned places, dislocated times—and uses them not to conjure horror but a much more deeply affecting sadness and sympathy.

Women's Weird 2 is rounded out by yet more excellent tales. Mary E. Wilkins Freeman shows us the strange realms that lie beyond even the most prosaic volumes of commonplace space in "The Hall Bedroom"; "The Black Stone Statue," by Mary Elizabeth Counselman, reveals how it is not always the monstrous that are the monsters. In fact, only "The Red Bungalow" fell slightly flat for me, with Bithia Mary Croker's evocative description of colonial India leading only to a disappointing "and then a scary thing happened" ending. This, though, is a mere matter of taste.

As a showcase of needlessly neglected stories from women writers, *Women's Weird 2* is as accomplished as its predecessor in both content and design. Again, Handheld Press offers useful biographical details and a glossary that helps with some of the more anachronistic terminology. Even more than this, as an exercise in describing the breadth of what the weird can achieve—not simply ghost stories or Gothic nightmares but, as Edmundson says, a way to "show us humanity at its best and worst and challenge us with meanings and messages that always fall somewhere between the explained and unexplained"—*Women's Weird 2* is a triumph.

Ramsey's Rant: The Urge to Splurge

Ramsey Campbell

Jacques Tourneur's *Night of the Demon* is my favourite horror film, and I'll cast no curse on the on-screen demon. Tourneur made it plain that he would have preferred not to show it, especially so early in the film, but for me it has always been inextricable from the total effect of the tale. I do see how Tourneur's version would have worked: the audience might have been gradually persuaded of the existence of the supernatural, as Dana Andrews' protagonist comes to be, whereas now we have to wait for him to learn what we already know. However, there's a sense in which the film (both the cut-down edit originally released and the later restoration) solves a different structural problem. Like Stoker's *Dracula* and several of the films of it, *Night of the Demon* shows its monster early on.

It's worth noting that both Stoker and Tourneur take care to build up a sense of dread and the uncanny before the initial revelation. In *The Beetle* (which began to see print in serial form a month after *Dracula* appeared) Richard Marsh brings on his monstrous insect in the first chapter, and Frank Belknap Long was to do the same in *The Horror from the Hills* with Chaugnar Faugn. In all these cases the early confrontation with the creature leaves its presence lurking behind the narrative, and the merest hint evokes it—less so in the Long, perhaps, which progressively abandons cosmic fear in favour of a mechanical solution. Let me note in passing Karl Freund's film *The Mummy,* the finest movie with that name, which—having given us an exemplary scene of terrible suggestiveness in the resurrection of the mummy—turns into an occult romance. All the other instances I've cited dispense with the need to construct a narrative that very gradually reveals the horror at its core, the classical method of Poe and Lovecraft. It may be argued that Stoker and the rest I've mentioned prefigure the use of prologues in many later stories, novels in particular, where the horror is at least partly shown in an opening chapter to whet the reader's appetite or placate the impatient. I'll admit it's possible to lose patience with (for instance) *The Door of the Unreal,* in which Gerald Biss spends most of a novel not quite revealing what the monster is. All the same, I think the structure Lovecraft developed has considerable merits, and I wouldn't like to see the field leave those behind.

Of course there are writers who come on as strong as they can from the outset and keep it up. In an early interview Clive Barker expresses dissatisfaction with having to wait for monsters in films only for them to prove to be men in rubber suits. The *Books of Blood* were his response, followed by *Hellraiser* and *Nightbreed*. Although at the time he said his first books aimed to terrify, I believe this has rarely engaged him as much as giving a voice to his monsters and celebrating otherness in the many gorgeous forms he creates for it. His method came to mind recently while I was writing a new tale, for the coda of which I considered having the unlucky victim of a painter's spectre end up squashed flat to fit into a mural. Clive could certainly have brought this off without disrupting the tone of a story of his, but in the context of mine it felt excessively fantastic, and it shows up as a dream instead.

Clive's tales can be excessive in the best way—explicit in a painterly sense—and his narrative construction is admirably sound. Other writers' structures can be rickety, not least some of mine. Most of my tales divide opinion, not least on Amazon. The late Joel Lane once described Amazon reviews as the place where literacy goes to die, and the hostile responses to my stuff that appear there are no more damning than the worst reviews of *The Great Gatsby,* say, or *Lord of the Flies*. I often reassure myself that way, but it won't do to dismiss them all. (I'm reminded how I originally dismissed Rob Latham's entirely reasonable analysis of *The Hungry Moon* in *Fantasy Review*.) *The Influence* has proved especially divisive, and not just on Amazon. I believe this is partly because it is itself divided. Some readers like the understated first section but find Rowan's homeward journey too explicitly uncanny, while others grow impatient with the book until it shifts into the other world. I've come to feel that the progression from suggestiveness to explicitness in a supernatural tale needs at least as much care as any other aspect of the narrative. It's a balance that can all too easily be lost, undermining if not destroying the mood and the conviction of the narrative. I fear this may have befallen *The Influence*.

I see a range of ways to ensure the balance doesn't totter. Lovecraft, as so often, tested all the methods he could use. The very gradual modulation of tone and detail in stories such as "The Rats in the Walls," "The Colour out of Space" and "The Call of Cthulhu" is exemplary. In "The Dunwich Horror" he finds a striking solution—showing us Wilbur Whateley's alien form in considerable scientific detail, having carefully built up to this disclosure, only to return to gathering suggestive elements towards a second confrontation, this one touching more on awe and dread. In a sense the method develops the device he used in "The Call of Cthulhu," having perhaps borrowed it from his recent reading of M. R. James' "Canon Alberic's Scrapbook," where a description of an image of the monster allows the appearance of the actual subject to be referred to rather than fully described.

I find abrupt lurches from reticence into explicitness especially unfortunate in film. I would even cite a favourite classic, Jacques Tourneur's *Cat People,* where the big cat in the office is a little too clearly visible for my taste, despite the director's contention that we only see a shadow. Up to this point the film has been fruitfully ambiguous, and the supernatural possibilities support rather than detract from the psychological. Perhaps after all the themes are interwoven strongly enough to survive this momentary lapse, if that's what it is. I'd argue that *Rosemary's Baby,* both book and film, preserves its ambiguity almost to the end by avoiding visual explicitness—by revealing the nature of the infant purely in the dialogue, and showing only Rosemary's reaction. Also maintained is the tone, which emphasises the banality of the Satanists all the way to the end. For me this consistency of tone helps the finale of *Hereditary,* where otherwise the film might feel suddenly overloaded with overstatement (though for some viewers it does). The deliberate progression of dread doesn't falter even when the revelations gather speed.

I tend to avoid comparisons, but two recent films are similar enough to invite them—the Norwegian *Babycall* (*The Monitor* in America) and the Australian *Babadook*. Central to both is a fraught relationship between a mentally disturbed single mother (in the Australian case a widow) and her young son, and both hint at the supernatural. Both grow less ambiguous or at any rate more explicit at the end. In *Babycall* it feels as if *Repulsion* reveals itself as a ghost story in the final reel. Both films convey disquiet for much of their length, not least in the familial relationship, and *The Babadook* boasts uncanny glimpses fully worthy of Val Lewton. It also suggests that not everything the mother sees is objectively real, but I for one had to invoke this insight very resolutely at the climax, which is so physical that it strains the explanation. More of Lewton's influence might have been helpful, and I'm left wondering to what extent explicitness is a required element in contemporary horror films, even if they maintain restraint for most of their length. Even music can overplay a scene. In *The Autopsy of Jane Doe,* overall a relentlessly effective piece, the episode in the corridor (which I won't spoil for those who haven't seen it) cries out for the Lewton method—the sound just of an approaching bell, not a crescendo on the soundtrack.

Lewton was reacting against the overstatement, as he saw it, of the Universal monster films. Perhaps we're due for a similar reaction, and in any case understatement never really leaves us. *The Blair Witch Project* is positively Lovecraftian, not just in espousing documentary realism but in accumulating fearful details that gather into inexplicit terror. The finale of *It Follows* may be controversial (though to my mind, however intelligent the young protagonists are, this doesn't mean their bid to defeat the supernatural threat need be any less ramshackle than our own might be) but the film overall shows no more than it has to, not least in daylight, and is the more unnerving for it. *The Borderlands* (*Final Prayer* in America) leads to an end that manages to be monstrously gruesome, not to mention claustrophobic, while showing almost no physical detail. *The Endless* (and *Resolution,* to which it's not so much a sequel as a parallel narrative) barely gives us a glimpse of its cosmic invader. At the very least, there's a heartening amount of subtlety about, which isn't to denigrate the graphic when it enriches the imagination. Here's to both modes when they do. There's more than enough room in our field for both.

Humperdinck Hansel development.

Sharpening a Dulled Blade: A Conversation with Jason Carney, Editor of *Whetstone*

Alex Houstoun

I have been struggling over the proper way to introduce this interview, and *Whetstone,* as a work for over a week. This is largely due to the fact that my own words feel overblown and unnecessary as compared to how *Whetstone* defines itself. *Whetstone* is a new amateur magazine that released its first issue this past spring; it seeks to "discover, inspire, and publish emerging authors who are enthusiastic about the tradition of 'pulp sword and sorcery.'"

Within this seemingly simple, direct definition of self, the first issue of *Whetstone* showcased an array of amateur talents that are both enthusiastic about traditional sword and sorcery but are also interested in exploring the limits of the genre. The magazine is simultaneously a welcome throwback and an invitation to look forward as to what sword and sorcery, or pulp generally, may be able to offer in the twenty-first century. This is emphasized by its online presence: whetstonemag.blogspot.com, a website that hosts issues of the magazine as well as reviews and reporting of notable works in the genre; twitter.com/SorceryWs, because who isn't on Twitter these days; and, perhaps most unique of all, a Discord channel meant to act as a digital forum and communal space for writers, critics, and general fans of the sword and sorcery tradition: discord.gg/ezEMRD4.

I was fortunate enough to exchange a series of emails with the magazine's editor, Jason Carney, to discuss the first issue of *Whetstone,* the inspirations and philosophies behind the magazine, and what the future may hold.

AH: What initially struck me about *Whetstone,* following the excellent cover art and Whetstone seal by Bill Cavalier, is the thesis you provide in the Editor's Note.

You write of being "suspicious of the arbitrary wall dividing the 'interpretation' and 'production' of literature," and also your astonishment at the large role played by *Weird Tales* as an institution—that is, the editors, readers, and writers—in the creation of the sword and sorcery genre. Literary art, you write, "requires the rich soil of a fecund artistic community."

It seems to me that *Whetstone* was created to serve two functions, that of a publication to showcase the works of writers in a particular genre and that of a community or, at least, a collaborative space in which editors, readers, and writers will presumably interact. Can you elaborate more on this dual role of *Whetstone* and how you came to develop this approach to creating the publication?

JC: First, thanks a lot for interviewing me. The staff and I are surprised and humbled by the response to *Whetstone*. We assumed we would have to solicit submissions in order to publish Issue 1. To the contrary, we were overwhelmed by submissions and had to pass on several great stories. There really is a wellspring of enthusiasm and talent for sword and sorcery.

Thanks for your comment about the editor's note! Brevity and sincerity were important for me there. But to your question. The idea that literary art is the product of singular geniuses who draw upon a finite cache of talent seems inaccurate. Analysis of *Weird Tales* does reveal that the key writers were in constant conversation with one another, their readers, their editors, and occasionally visual artists. They read one another's works. They discussed what they were reading. And they allowed for serendipity in their discussions. For example, consider the intriguing correspondence between Robert E. Howard and H. P. Lovecraft, where they debated the merits and shortcomings of civilization and barbarism. That conversation is intriguing, sometimes silly, other times profound. Without a doubt this conversation allowed the writers to articulate and hone philosophical views, and those views enriched their work. But there's more: Howard initially connected with Lovecraft through a fan letter. His fan letter was sent to Lovecraft by the editor of *Weird Tales,* Farnsworth Wright. Wright was one of the first editors to pay Howard for his writing, i.e., to authorize Howard to think of himself as a professional writer. Finally, there is the issue of *Weird Tales,* the magazine, the overall print publication enterprise that brought Howard, Wright, and Lovecraft together.

From a wide enough angle, the emergence of sword and sorcery in *Weird Tales* was a function of collective human activity, not singular genius. The creation of sword and sorcery was not only a matter of Howard's talent, his unique vision. As much as I like the term "the creator of sword and sorcery," it is inaccurate. Sword and sorcery didn't have a single creator, a father, per se. It wasn't a child, a cohesive exuda. A better analogy would be to consider sword and sorcery as a "chemical reaction" and all the various entities "reagents." Howard was a key reagent, perhaps the "main" reagent, if you will, but there were several other reagents.

What does this have to do with *Whetstone*? I am acquainted with many fans, scholars, and deep readers of sword and sorcery who do not consider themselves creative writers. I think they are wrong. We are all creative writers because we are all humans and all humans are storytellers. And yet, I don't blame my friends for diminishing themselves by refuting this inextricable part of their humanity. Why? I think the current aesthetic conditions conspire against them. It seems we are often asked to choose one role and stick to it: (1) writer or (2) deep reader. I will not test your patience by rehearsing the history of modern literary criticism, but let it suffice to say that the idea of a critic, a humanities technician, or journalist who studies or reviews literature and does not also create it is a new and toxic phenomenon. For me, the book-life has been tragically fragmented by late capitalism's demand for narrower and narrower forms of specialization and technical expertise. Thinking, reading, writing: these are not distinct processes but instead facets of the same type of aesthetic activity. As far as *Whetstone* is specifically concerned: the low word count, the frontloaded amateur status, the free and open access digital distribution models—these are strategic choices to raise any barriers to anyone who wants to write sword and sorcery. We want *Whetstone* to be the reason you no longer have an excuse to put off trying your hand at spinning a tale of high adventure, skullduggery, eldritch sorcery, and crumbling ruins . . .

AH: I must confess it is hard not to read your final sentence as a rather exciting and ambitious exclamation. I am all for it!

The mention of *Weird Tales* and connection and community via fan letters has me curious: do you have plans for a letters page in future issues of *Whetstone*? How do you envision the publication fostering a community? Do you see your role as something akin to Wright in that you passively connect one writer to another in passing along messages, or do you hope to build something more substantive in which parties will be able to facilitate their own connections?

JC: I haven't considered having a fan letter section, but thank you for the great idea! I love how each pulp magazine had a thematically appropriate title for their fan letter sections. We are familiar with "The Eyrie" in *Weird Tales*. I also enjoy *Adventure* magazine's letter page, "The Camp-Fire." What would be an appropriate letters page title for *Whetstone*? What could I call it? I digress! One way we hope to foster a community around *Whetstone* is, of course, through typical social media outlets, but a more atypical move we made was to set up a Discord server. If readers are not familiar with Discord, it is an app for hosting private chat servers. Many of the writers published in the first issue of *Whetstone* joined the server, and so far we have had interesting conversations about sword and sorcery required reading, brainstorming about plot and character development, and, of course, fun debates about our favorite writers. A link to join the *Whetstone* Discord Server is on our webpage. All are welcome!

As regards my role: I am reluctant to cast myself in the role of a Wright! What a legacy! There are, however, certain figures in the burgeoning sword and sorcery revival who serve as critical nexus points. Seth Lindberg, for example, hosts an active Goodreads sword and sorcery reading group; DMR Books, a sword-and-sorcery-focused press, releases a weekly blog aggregate to direct attention to sword-and-sorcery-related blog posts. And there are extremely kind and generous writers in the genre who respond to fans and function as mentors for many of us (although I am not sure if they think of themselves in this way). There are two generous writers whom I want to highlight in this regard: (1) David C. Smith, author of the great *Oron* classic sword and sorcery novels, who is producing new work; and (2) Howard Andrew Jones, author of several critically acclaimed sword and sorcery novels, such as *For the Killing of Kings*. David C. Smith has corresponded with me about sword and sorcery for over a year now, and his long, well-crafted emails are examples of classic authorial epistolary elegance. Howard Andrew Jones and I have had wide-ranging literary conversations over the phone about sword and sorcery and literary history, and he has provided a treasure map of a reading list. One final person I should mention is the sword and sorcery historian Brian Murphy, whose *Flame and Crimson: A History of Sword-and-Sorcery* has been read by many of us; it is really a wonderful introduction to the genre. I may not be Wright, but we have the equivalent of a Wright in writers orbiting the community, and we are thankful for them. An obvious element of the community is its homogeneity, so I fully accept, as one of my key responsibilities, cultivating hospitality to difference. I can start on that now: let me take the occasion of this interview to extend a *Whetstone* invitation to amateur writers of diverse backgrounds, genders, and colors!

AH: Would "The Strop" be suitable for a letter section? Is that too obvious?

While you may be reluctant to cast yourself in the role of a Wright, you do take a proactive approach to being an editor. By this I mean, in addition to the Editor's Note, you include an introduction and commentary to each piece. Personally, I appreciated the introductions as they provide nice setups as to the mindset and approach the reader should take with each story.

At the same time, I noticed what felt a little bit like a tension: you offer comparisons to some of the forerunners of the genre—of the ten stories, three are compared to Robert E.

Howard, Fritz Leiber, and Clark Ashton Smith, respectively, along with references to how others reflect on traditions of the genre—but you also appear to be suggesting that these stories do a little more, that they build upon the genre. You also just noted the homogeneity of the community. It seems to me that part of the goal of *Whetstone* is to showcase work that both revels and celebrates sword and sorcery while also trying to expand upon what the reader may expect of the genre. Is this a fair analysis?

JC: It's gratifying to know that my editorial introductions for *Whetstone* 1 were interesting. I had fun writing them. As an amateur genre writer, it is important to have one's work contextualized within the broader tradition, even if, ultimately, one seeks to leave that tradition behind completely. And it's always fun to see one's name next to a writer who inspired you. My success condition for literary criticism is to direct readers' attention to otherwise obscure facets of a work that they may not have been aware of; that was certainly what I was going for in *Weird Tales of Modernity,* my academic book on pulp fiction. Inversely, I think literary criticism fails when it buries works beneath the tendentious observations of the critic. Put simply, literary criticism should be a lens to see clearer with and not a distorting funhouse mirror.

I agree that there is a tension between hewing to a previous sword and sorcery tradition and wanting to innovate in the genre, to take it into new territory, to bring in new writers, and to reach new readers. There is also the related tension between the genre's roots in pulp spectacle entertainment and my desire to take it seriously as a form of literary art. One wants to pay homage to the sword and sorcery tradition but not to rehearse the same tired plots and project insularity; one wants to write entertaining stories in the pulp tradition, but tenaciously hewing to that tradition often comes from a genuine place of serious aesthetic fascination. How to proceed? Alas, I don't think these tensions can be completely resolved. Nevertheless, as editor of *Whetstone,* I am on the lookout for sword and sorcery stories that seek to harmonize these tensions, that celebrate sword and sorcery while also making it new. For example, a story in *Whetstone* 1 that really rang my bell was Géza A. G. Reilly's "The Wizard's Demise." This story took place in a sorcerer's tower and featured the conventional sorcerer villain and barbarian warrior protagonist; however, the narrative was from the sorcerer's point of view. I won't spoil how the story ends, but it was a refreshing inversion of the conventional sword and sorcery trope of the barbarian warrior as protagonist. Reilly's tale skillfully nodded to the sword and sorcery tradition while also invigorating it. On a more logistical level, however, we have had difficulty getting submissions from women and writers of color, and doing so, I think, is essential for widening the readership of sword and sorcery. Recognition of Self and experience is one of the great joys of reading, after all. I have personally invited such writers to submit and certainly hope they do!

AH: There seem to be opposite aesthetic or literary philosophies at work. You write of your desire, and perhaps the desire of many other amateur genre writers, to be contextualized within a genre's traditions while also pushing beyond the genre itself. You then note that writers of the genre seemingly have to make a choice between the genre's roots in pulp spectacle and a choice to use the genre as a form of literary art. One can write a fine literary piece that plays with the settings of sword and sorcery but is not entirely true to the genre, or one can write a piece that is sword and sorcery but has no greater intellectual or artistic weight . . . Perhaps I am misunderstanding the situation? Can you elaborate on these tensions and the potential inability to resolve them? Are there works that come close within the genre, or is this one of those paradox-of-writing situations that will forever spur authors toward an attempt and subsequent failure?

JC: I can understand why it might seem that these aesthetic philosophies are opposite; and I acknowledge that they are attitudes in intellectual competition, in charged tension. I should be clear, though: I completely disagree with the idea that writers should feel compelled to resolve this joyful tension by making a choice. When I say the tension can be left unresolved I imagine an ideal writer who (1) hews to sword and sorcery tradition—knows their Lovecraft, Howard, Leiber, Vance, and Moorcock—and (2) innovates sword and sorcery *at the same time*. Is this a koan? Am I trying to have my Hyborian pastry and eat it too? Maybe. Alas, this issue, this knot, is the perennial problem in literature, and, in general, publishers/editors have so much less agency in this realm than writers and readers, of course. A publisher can provide a supported forum for innovation to happen; and an editor can authorize innovative writers by championing and publishing them; ultimately, however, readers (and critics) have a final say in what they enjoy, in what they judge to be successful, entertaining, and worthwhile. This is why it is important for me to keep *Whetstone* a non-commercial enterprise. Being liberated from commercial concerns brings with it a valuable amount of artistic freedom. In the early twentieth century (a period I am enthralled by as a literary historian), so much innovative literature "happened" because it was liberated from the necessity of pleasing bottom-line anxious publishers and editors and unadventurous, trope-seeking readers. The so-called "little magazines" of Modernism published the experimental works of James Joyce, Ezra Pound, T. S. Eliot, and F. T. Marinetti, and were able to do so simply because they didn't seek advertisers in their pages. *Whetstone* is open for "ads/bulletins," but we don't charge for them. Our "ad-space" is gratis, our magazine is free, and therefore we are under no obligation to make a compromise with the unadventurous reader of sword and sorcery. To return to a final part of your question: I love the way you write, "This sounds like one of those paradox-of-writing situations that will forever spur authors forward," and I think that is correct. You make me want to triangulate three theories of literary literary innovation and champion one above the other two: (1) there is a the *radical innovator,* the futurist who wants to forget the old books, the canon, and maybe set them on fire, and write new and better ones; (2) there is the reactionary preservationist/pastichist, the classicist, the writer who wants to hew closely, even obsessively, to previously established canons and conventions; and then there is the wonderful third option, (3) the triangulator, who reads deeply in the literary tradition, works in response to that tradition, and nevertheless produces a new work of art that responds to that tradition, changes it, electrifies it, and brings in new readers by making it less insular. Lest I get carried away, let me acknowledge that my role is a small one: all I can do as a publisher and editor is to look for those triangulators and praise them when they emerge. They are a rare breed, but I was lucky to publish a few in *Whetstone* 1.

AH: Your comments about the "little magazines" of yore and *Whetstone* being a non-commercial enterprise raise a subject I was hoping to find a natural way to segue into . . . thanks! The presentation of *Whetstone,* in no small part thanks to Cavalier's art, is definitely a throwback and made me think of the fanzines or a tattered pulp magazine that I used to buy from a local record store. Looking at the cover, I felt I should have found this publication on a shelf that is barely standing next to a poorly put-together punk zine and maybe a few Ballantine anthologies that have seen better days. And yet, the actual thing I was reading was a PDF on a tablet.

I acknowledge that there is definitely an ease and accessibility to making a digital publication, but can you speak about the thought process and preparation for making *Whetstone* digital? Is a physical publication something you envision for the future? Does the desire to keep *Whetstone* non-commercial essentially prevent the cost and labor that comes with printing a work? Finally, if I can get really faux-deep, what does it mean to you to curate and create a non-commercial work? Is it simply the refusal to attach a price to the publication and the decision not to seek out or be driven by profit?

JC: I love the comparison between indie zines and *Whetstone*. Cavalier's art reminds me of two kinds of "independent" art: the early-era role-playing art in Advanced Dungeons and Dragons books and the awesomely bizarre indie "gig" posters of the 1980s that were stapled on bar walls and posts around Columbus, Ohio, where I grew up. So the "raw" quality of counter-culture print was something I was going for in *Whetstone*'s design.

To your question about digital distribution and curating non-commercial work: apologies for getting philosophical here! When an artistic enterprise isn't obligated to a commercial investment, interesting things can start to happen (sometimes good and sometimes bad). Arguably, financial investment in an artistic enterprise can assure quality, though several overfunded Hollywood productions will give the lie to that claim. Nevertheless, the really experimental, avant-garde literature of the interwar period became elitist and inhospitable to general readers because it was not beholden to a business office. That's a similar kind of shame as the corporate-sponsored blockbuster that bombs. Can we find a sweet spot? This is a complicated issue for us. Print-on-demand technology makes transforming a PDF into a print book convenient and free, but we decided against it, because when you print something you can no longer distribute it gratis without losing money. So it wasn't simply the cost of printing that made us prefer digital to print distribution but instead our desire to make it available gratis. We want *Whetstone* to be truly and sincerely "amateur," i.e., "for the love of it," and that seemed to require being able to just give it away to those interested. We sometimes forget "amateur" doesn't necessarily mean "not professional." We also sometimes forget that if you sell art, something sinister always happens: it becomes a commodity. A cynical person might say that once you sell art it stops being art and instead becomes a mere commodity. I'm not sure I'd go that far, but the argument is at least pausing over. Why? I do believe that this commodification process necessarily authorizes the consumer to make demands on you, and often unreasonable ones. Put crudely: we wanted to inoculate ourselves against discouraging, morale-destroying criticism, and not selling *Whetstone* helps in this way. If *Whetstone* sucks, no one can really complain. It's free! It's amateur! It's digital! This is so liberating for a hesitant and amateur writer entering the crucible of the public demonstration. Not only does it authorize amateur writers to take changes, it kind of starts the conversation in a critically hospitable zone (we hope). We currently do not have plans for a print version, but we have been queried by a couple of independent presses about it.

AH: So, with this guiding philosophy, where does *Whetstone* go from this first issue? How does it go? Does it grow or change? You had mentioned a Discord server and fostering a community, and I imagine things are developing the release of this first issue, so what comes next in planning the next issue?

JC: First things first: we need to produce high-quality issues. We are proud of Issue 1. We are currently finishing Issue 2. [The second issue appeared December 4th, 2020—ED.] And we are making plans for Issue 3. These three issues are our foundation. Whatever happens in terms of the orbiting community, we will nevertheless focus our attention firmly on our central condition of success: inspiring, discovering, and showcasing the work of new and amateur writers of sword and sorcery. What comes after that? It's a secret.

AH: A publication committed to pushing the limits of a genre, bringing new work to light, and with secret plans in the future . . . sounds like the start of an interesting story!

To end things on a light note: what have you been reading lately?

JC: Thanks! I'm currently reading Eric Hobsbawn's, *The Age of Extremes: A History of the World, 1914–1991,* Charles Saunders's *Imaro,* Stacy Schiff's history of the Salem witch trials, *The Witches: Salem, 1692,* and a bunch of overwrought academic stuff! Let me also say I just finished Howard Andrew Jones's *The Desert of Souls,* an S&S novel set in medieval Baghdad. It was excellent, a masterful model for future novel-length treatments of sword and sorcery.

"A Monstrous Rhapsody on Otherness"

Jerome Winter

JAMES GOHO. *Caitlín R. Kiernan: A Critical Study of Her Dark Fiction*. Jefferson, NC: McFarland, 2020. 206 pp. $39.95 tpb. ISBN: 978-1-4766-8089-7.

By the latest tally, a writer of over a dozen well-respected novels, and over a hundred and fifty critically acclaimed short stories, and winner of numerous prestigious awards, including two Bram Stoker and World Fantasy Awards, Caitlín R. Kiernan certainly deserves the recognition of a book-length study of her fiction. Enter James Goho's compellingly researched and cogently written book, which breaks relatively fresh academic ground as the first major critical overview of Kiernan's daunting oeuvre, a study sweepingly selective and wide-ranging in scope, but also couched in grainy, close, and saturated readings, all inflected by an eclectic but insightful set of theoretical perspectives on the urban horror, dark-fantasy, and New Weird subgenres. Although produced by a single able critic and about a single author, the taxonomy found in these pages reads more like an anthology of various contributors with minimal transitional continuity or structuring between or across chapters beyond the baseline notion that Kiernan's peculiar brand of weirdness frequently deconstructs, transforms, and reimagines standard horror tropes for marginal, queer, and outcast perspectives such that her stories often become a "monstrous rhapsody on otherness." Therefore, the study's bug of being multifariously organized turns out to be a design feature, given Kiernan's status as not only an unusually polymorphous, prolific, and protean artist but also bearing in mind that the living writer has an ongoing publication schedule, which will possibly remain vibrant for decades yet to come.

The first chapter, "The Call of the Sí," argues that Kiernan, born in Ireland, reworks Gothic motifs from a distinctively

Irish perspective. Goho follows postcolonial literary theorists such as Aoife Dempsey and Declan Kiberd to argue that modern Irish literature invokes the terrifying, child-abducting faerie and howling, deathly women of Irish folklore to write back fiercely against the corrosive historical effects of colonization on the island. Specifically, Goho argues that Kiernan's story "Stoker's Mistress" (1996) deploys a vampiric version of the *leannán sídhe* figure of folklore to inspire Bram Stoker to bear witness to the disease, famine, and bloodshed that produces both the nightmare of colonial Irish history and the foundational horror novel *Dracula* (1897). Likewise, in "Emptiness Spoke Eloquent" (1997), Kiernan resists the invasion anxiety of the metropole by transforming Mina Harker into the monstrous revenge of repressed Irish rage, as she conducts an urbane murder spree across an already devastated early twentieth-century Europe. The second chapter, "Kiernan Echoes the Literary Decadence," segues into Kiernan's recycling of Wildean fin-de-siècle tropes in general, including the taboo-busting violation of earnest moralizing, the enshrining of the artistic aura in a crassly commercial age, an obsession with the allure of the dilapidated, and a reclaiming of illicit queer desire. Indeed, Kiernan's work regularly depicts dark lesbian romances, such as the disturbing one in "Derma Sutra (1891)," set in a mythologized Wild West of American history, where such proscribed pleasure dangerously flouts the reigning patriarchal and heteronormative status quo of then and now.

The compelling third chapter, "The Figure of the Gothic Body," examines four ways Kiernan explores the trauma, fragility, and abjection of the physiological, existential body in her Gothic fiction: namely, the body as tortured, the body stigmatized as "disabled," the body as transgender, and the body as melancholic. All these readings are lucid and illuminating. For instance, Goho argues that Kiernan's "The Steam Dancer (1896)" (2007) both updates C. L. Moore's "No Woman Born" (1944) and resists disability theorist Rosemarie Garland-Thomson's notion of "the supercrip," or the exceptional disability narrative, in its story of Missouri Banks, whose arm and leg cyborg prosthetics and work as an exotic dancer are not fetishized but humanly rendered. Likewise, Goho cogently contends that Kiernan's haunting "The Ammonite Violin (Murder Ballad No. 4)" (2006) reflects the harrowing depths of terminal depression from the perspective of a suicidal serial killer who has gruesomely converted his last victim's body into a violin that the victim's sister plays to cathartically release her own stalled mourning. The fourth chapter, "The Folklore of Awe and Terror," returns to Kiernan's rewritings of the oral storytelling tradition of fairy tales, but this time viewing the stories as allegories for environmental devastation. Hence Goho interprets the ways Kiernan's novel *The Red Tree* deploys the trappings of a haunted secluded farm narrative to make more sweeping eco-Gothic commentary on the eerie, apocalyptic estrangement of living in the Anthropocene era.

Chapter Five, "Warnings to the Curious," explores a signal aspect of Kiernan's role as exemplar of what is sometimes called the New Weird in fiction; that is, her preoccupation with the maddening intrusion of inexplicable, unnamable entities that defy classification. Methodically excavating unpredictable alien monsters from deep time comes easily to Kiernan, who has been a practicing paleontologist. It should therefore come as no surprise that quite a few of her stories, such as "Blind Fish" (2012), "The Bone's Prayer" (2009), and "Nor the Demons Down under the Sea" (2002), revolve around salvaging uncanny fossils from the primeval past. Likewise, in Chapter Six, "Haunted Perceptions," Goho argues that Kiernan's characters who perceive seemingly supernatural dimensions of existence are nevertheless engaging with the material world that contradicts not only conventional religious or cultural realities but the known physical and biological laws of the universe. Hence, in the cosmically weird "Ex Libris," Maggie Ellen Morse metamorphoses into an eldritch horror after being exposed to a fungal infection from a box of baleful books; in "Tidal Forces" and "The Hole with a Girl in its Heart" (2007), people mysteriously grow transdimensional black holes inside their bodies. The scientifically minded might quibble and cavil at the sheer absurdity of this weird fiction; however, that hallucinatory violation of scientific paradigms is exactly Kiernan's desired effect. Goho performs a superb tracing of how this New Weird subgenre protocol works in a wide variety of Kiernan's work.

Then, Chapter Seven, "Spectral Hauntings," shifts from the cosmic weird to postmodern fiction with extended exegesis of *The Red Tree* (2009) and perhaps Kiernan's greatest novel, *The Drowning Girl: A Memoir* (2012). Goho argues that these stories cannily exploit the hauntology of spectral-visitation narratives to deconstruct the confessional mode of storytelling. Chapter Eight, "Dark Futures," concerns Kiernan's science fiction, especially her future fiction written in a dystopian vein. The chapter includes a detailed dissection of her novella *Dry Salvages* (2004), which Goho considers an "anti-space opera," a gritty, thinly veiled reverse-colonization narrative about encountering infectious exobiology set in a spacefaring totalitarian state of the regrettably plausible far future. In the ninth chapter, "Retruthing Steampunk," Goho argues that Kiernan's steampunk fiction cuts against the normative grain of the subgenre by offering a sustained critique of the patriarchal, imperialist, and capitalist presumptions of the subgenre. Goho book then ends insightfully with a final summative concluding chapter.

This study is not without minor flaws that nevertheless warrant mentioning. There are, for instance, some cursory, undeveloped references to stories or novels that ostensibly demonstrate a probing theoretical insight, but the reader is left to take the author's word for it; there are also some overgeneralized representations of complex fields of academic discourse, such as the reductive take on Science and Technology Studies (STS) as categorically subscribing to post-truth anti-science beliefs and colluding with conservative climate-change denialism; and, although more amply informed by sparring debates in the field of SF criticism, there is similarly an unconvincing burning of straw-man caricatures of some vast bodies of contemporary fiction, such as the previously mentioned generalized dismissal of the entire steampunk subgenre, regrettably tarring a variegated spate of wildly different and complex works of literature, fashion, music, film, and art with the same toxic brush. However, in the final interpretative reward of the chapters, none of these peccadillos that pertain merely to matters of emphasis and degree add up to a fatal Achilles' heel for the study or drastically undercut its larger central case of carefully and critically attending to the astonishing significance and eclectic range of Kiernan's dark fiction.

Ambiguous to a Fault

Géza A. G. Reilly

MICHAEL GRIFFIN. *Armageddon House*. Pickering, ON: Undertow Publications, 2020. 124 pp. $12.00 tpb. ISBN: 978-1-988964-20-1.

What would the psychological impact of immortality be? What would the end of the world mean to an immortal? What are the limits of identity, and are they as mutable as bodies are? These are all questions that are raised by Michael Griffin's novella *Armageddon House*. Unfortunately, while these questions are engaging, ambiguity plagues Griffin's slim offering, making the whole less palatable than it could otherwise have been. Answers aren't always needed to make a weird work satisfying, it's true, but I'm left feeling that Griffin's narrative can't support the almost arthaus effect he seems to be going for.

Armageddon House is what it says on the tin: It's the story of four people—survivors of some kind—who are trapped within a massive, ultramodern structure that runs from cavernous bedrock up to an opulent museum beside a titanic sealed door. These people, Mark, Jenna, Polly, and Greyson, have been trapped in the structure for so long that their knowledge of who they are and what the state of the world is has become slippery and inconsistent. If there is a reason why they're all here, they can't name it, and thus they go through their daily routines—eating, drinking, exercising, sunbathing, arguing, and mating—in a constant atmosphere of confused monotony. Individuals shuck both flesh and histories like snakeskin, disappearances and reappearances are common, and changes are both constant and seemingly inconsequential. The questions of how long they've been stuck in this ultra-modern ark and why are they the only ones are often voiced but never resolved.

This is all promising fare, on the surface of it, and if *Armageddon House* were dialed slightly differently in one direction or the other, I would have enjoyed it far more. The narrative could have easily been either a gripping post-apocalyptic tale of disintegrating personalities and the fracturing of humanity—and possibly more—under stress *or* a sprawling epic with deep, meaningful questions about history and metaphysics. Unfortunately, *Armageddon House* is ultimately dialed in neither of those directions, and as a result everything becomes an interesting, but failed, experiment.

The central problem with Griffin's work is the ambiguity that runs through the novella from start to finish. As I've said, ambiguity can be fine within a weird work, but Griffin's intense refusal to answer the questions that he's set out almost reaches the level of student-film parody. There are no answers nor any definitive statements in these pages, and upon exiting the narrative the reader is left only to wonder what it had all *meant*. I'm all for stories that require deep, personal interpretation, but I generally find that there has to be *something* definitive in a work upon which an interpretation can be hung. *Armageddon House,* instead, proposes one particular answer, but that answer is fouled by the fact that it makes *every other aspect of the narrative more confusing*. Rather than culminating in its disparate pieces coming together, even if only through suggestion, the ending of the novella instead causes the whole to fall apart into a confusing morass.

This is not to say that *Armageddon House* is "bad," which I am loath to call any book without serious cause. Indeed, Griffin's construction of his microcosmic world is compelling, often frightening, and capable of inspiring awe in the reader. His characters, too, are interesting, believable, and engaging enough to make the reader continue turning the pages. It's just that the whole, when taken as the sum of its parts, is intensely *frustrating,* and not in the invigorating way that other ambiguous or subtle projects might be. But for all that I wanted to hurl *Armageddon House* across the room after finishing it, I did keep *thinking* about it, which is not something I can say about every book that isn't to my taste. If only it had captivated my attention *and* ultimately been possessed of a satisfying through-line in its story, I would not hesitate to recommend it.

I've been trying to avoid spoilers in this review, but I don't think I can any longer. If you'd like to read *Armageddon House* unspoiled, and I don't think I can quite say that's a bad idea, skip the rest of this paragraph. Otherwise, here's my bone of contention: the "secret" at the heart of the narrative seems to be that the four inhabitants of the shelter are, in some way, gods—probably from the Norse pantheon. Ragnarök has happened, and the gods are living it, transforming again and again in their isolation. Unsure about whether they should go on living in the shelter (which seems to be both Ragnarök and part of the world-tree Yggdrasil), Mark, newly woken up to the knowledge of what he and his compatriots are, is saved from . . . something . . . by marble statues of a man and a woman, who seem to be Ash and Embla, the first humans created by the gods. Rather than embracing a renewal of this perpetual apocalypse, however, Mark decides to shoot himself and the other three survivors-cum-gods and see what happens after that—if anything *can* happen after that. Whether he succeeds or not is left up to the reader, leaving a cherry on top of all the other unanswered questions. If this is a perpetual Ragnarök embedded in the roots of Yggdrasil . . . why is the shelter not Norse, not particularly godly for that matter, and entirely modern? What has actually happened, and are the survivors really the gods that they seem to be? The facility is obviously built to hold more survivors, presumably gods, so where are they? Why are the survivors drifting away from their higher selves as their deaths are continually denied?

This all leaves the sense of having walked out of a movie and, with a shrug of one's shoulders, having no other reaction than saying "Okay. What?" Michael Griffin clearly likes big ideas, and he has an interesting method of implementing those ideas. However, his decision to keep answers so tantalizingly out of reach to the reader so consistently doesn't elevate the narrative: it dissolves it into incomprehensibility. I don't think that *Armageddon House* is *bad*, but I don't think that I can recommend it to anyone other than those who are intrigued by the second paragraph of this review. Or, I suppose, to those who enjoy being tantalized without being satisfied.

A Trade in Futures
Part II.
Dan Raskin

The Exchange Terminus is where all classifications of organics congregate. Resources are acquired or discarded amid the whirring, blinking apparatuses that conduct exchange functions for the Complex. There are rules and norms that regulate this activity. Cheating, stealing, argumentation, and conflict also occur. Any value realized though exchanges by organics is rapidly metabolized back into the Complex so that it does not multiply and accrue. The recluse faces the grim wall that encloses the Terminus and considers how the leaking mutations patterning his legs can be exchanged for his desired extinction. Never before has he imagined a beneficiary of his investment. The concept of "desire" applied to an entity other than himself fills him with queasiness. Yet a sensation swells from his legs that confirms the value latent in his degenerate limbs.

Entering the Terminus involves pressing oneself against a smooth riveted surface and reaching into a ventilation duct to pull a lever. This signals that someone outside is seeking admission. On the occasion of admittance, which is what happens for the recluse at this time, there follows a flurry of events involving flashing colored lights, loss of peripheral vision, and procedural inquiries followed by a skeptical acceptance of credentials. His memories of previous attempts, and his ingrown wariness of others, grant him a degree of preparation for this generalized disorientation.

The structural layout of the Terminus has always been baffling to the recluse. What the recluse recalls but cannot clearly perceive is that the avenues and passages of the Terminus spill out in all directions from a central tunnel, larger and more spacious than the one that carried him here. In the first period of settlement in Complex, organics had found this to be among the most spacious and least dangerous places to congregate. The seemingly endless maze of tracks, and the mad proliferation of crevasses and halls for freight storage, created an environment perfect for chance encounters, private meetings, curious meanderings, and clandestine trade. And yet, the constant movement of freight prevented any truly permanent inhabitation. The history and prior uses of the Terminus are somehow known to him as matters of fact. He has only known it as a place of trade.

As he turns from the matte screen that has administered his credentials test, his is superseded by an unforeseen aspect of experience. In the empty slots of his perception, an oily imprint takes form, as if a liquid seep from a hidden spot on the wall had swollen through his garments and onto his skin before he thought to distinguish the salty dampness of his endogenous secretions from the warm slick of this secret source-fluid. The imprint pools and soon exceeds the emptiness and spills into awareness. A thought, or narrative secretion, occurs that jolts him into a queasy physicality: *Vicars know and want what I have brought to sell.* Previously, when he thought of the vicars and their vague functions, he could rely on the fact of his irrelevance to subdue the dread that accompanied the knowledge of their presumed existence. But now this blackened oily leakage from behind his mind acts as a surfactant, separating the fact of his irrelevance from the fact of the vicars. A mute terror seizes him and forces him toward the inopportune bustle of the Terminus.

In his immediate state of fear, his capacity to receive and process any but the barest determinants of order is severely blurred. Another rare expression of compatibility between himself and the world, he notices. Emerging from the lilted shuffling of undefined figures, from the orderly passage of carriage and freight, from the hazy sheen melting off each blurred surface, a dissonant cacophony of muted sound bores into his ears. Fear draws his faculties downwards, settling in the hidden glyphs encircling his legs. An alert tightness takes hold in his legs and draws him into the blur. He lurches forward. After several steps he reaches to the ground to smudge grease, dust, or any available particulate onto his fingers, which he then tongues with a seeking need. He tastes only his fingertips, and he accepts that the clean floor of the Terminal cannot provide him with the necessary distraction. He proceeds.

Grim voices pierce through the cacophony from underlit nooks and corners, slipping momentarily into clarity. "Why not buy another voice for you to hear when you are defunct?" . . . "Know what it was like here before we discovered the new deep material—an unregulated environment in heaving chaos!" . . . "There are still thousands like you, flung tragically from the system. Recall yourself and you'll receive a bit-wallet *and* a registered dwelling!" The neon hisses of these vendors elicit only the mildest curiosity in the recluse. But as he hobbles into the clamor of the Terminus, he begins to sense that the content of these whispers suggests shared desires and requirements of other organics in the Complex—that they snake and seethe across the boundaries of what could be called "society." In his certainty about most things being chronically absent, he somehow feels innately confident in the fact of his irrelevance. It is far from him to formulate the question of who or what he is irrelevant to. But from this understanding, he begins to accept that these secretive hissings demarcate his very existence, however distantly. And so he continues to listen and to follow what he hears.

Guided by the directives of some poorly defined impulse, the recluse chooses one of the many passages to enter, where he can walk unimpeded underneath hanging tracks upon which crates of unknowable materials glide silently. He turns into another, which leads slightly downwards, and into yet another. The sensory tumult of the central tunnel has long diminished into a flat-textured hum, and vendors decrease in frequency as inhabitable nooks become scarcer. Though his legs are fully exhausted and numb, they tremble when a solicitous whisper calls out from either the right or the left.

"Returns on long investments! Free prospecting, guaranteed payoff starting at tier three." The whisperer, perhaps sensing something distinct in the recluse's gait, quickly adds: "For tiers one and two, offers of dissolution, expansion, or pressurization are available."

The forward momentum in his legs ceases without his awareness, and the recluse halts. "I want to descend." He coughs into the dim glow of the passage.

A pause. "Doable," replies the whisper. "Let me grade them."

A figure emerges from a shadow and greets the recluse with a slight nod of its head, which is adorned with ocular scopes and topped with thin hair and unruly flakes of skin. The recluse stands dumbly for a moment, mouth agape. Then he attempts to recite the routine that has until only recently defined his existence. To express a past happening, or sequence of happenings, or the gray fog of boredom regularly punctuated with such happenings requires an ordered and differentiated conception of activity. Instead, words fall out of his mouth in muciileal chunks. "My investment . . . galvanized . . . incubated . . . daily at least."

"Good, good. Typical protocol, I see. Step in here with me to my workshop." The figure eyes the recluse cannily. "Your fingers? No . . . arms are unmodified as well. Feet? Legs? Torso?" The recluse bends forward and lifts the cloth that covers his legs, revealing the inflamed webbing that creeps up past his knees. "Legs! Delightful, yes. There is a particular *density* to what can be achieved with the legs that . . . well, never mind. Come, come please." The prospector gestures toward a bench set into the darkness. The recluse lays upon it.

"Do you know why you arrived here? Some do, many don't. I am merely curious, as this is rather a specialty prospecting station. So far out of the way and all." The prospector locates the socket between the recluse's ribs and fits into it a thick greased cable. The recluse feels a charge surge through his torso. The prospector then begins handling a large-screened tablet, tuning its settings and scanning it quickly up and down the bare legs of the recluse, who is silent. "No? Fine, that is fine. You seem to know at least something of your intention. Perhaps you shall get your descent. Many do not qualify. Now let me assess this . . . composition." The tablet emits a silent glow as it glides over the glistening folds of his rash.

The whispers and hissing static that had trailed the recluse during his blurred commute have ceased, and in this quiet he locates the spectral hum of the tablet. It crowds the recluse's senses like a dusty fog until there is nothing else but it and the tense current enervating his weak musculature. The humming modulates in inverted overtones with the subcutaneous sigils of his legs. Vicious harmonics vibrating the surface rash and burrowing into the fractal architecture. Amidst threaded columns of inflamed tissue, raving auricles intertwined, rigid and frictionless shafts, the hum resonates with the mutant glyphs. Thus amplified, the hum is given texture and mass. It seethes back outwards. Oily and viscous, it clings to the desiccated particulates that comprise this sensory void. The humming begins to condense and differentiate into a voice, or an echo of many simultaneous voices. It is the voice of the vicars, channeled into the recluse's pitiable awareness. The recluse cannot know what they seek to communicate, but their knowledge of their avarice is inescapable. The Complex is theirs, and all within must eventually feed its hunger. The recluse's totalizing inhabitation within this terrible caucus persists until the tablet is turned off and the humming evaporates. The voices recede and his memory drains into the folds of his rash until all that remains is a lingering dread and a desperation to dispose of his embodied cargo.

The prospector carefully sets down the tablet and watches the recluse emerge from his trance. "The quality of mutations . . . high. Very high. Exquisite patterning. Among the most delicate and intriguing I have encountered. The readings indicate nearly complete muscular penetration . . . quite rare."

There is a dumb satisfaction in learning the prospector's final grade for his investment. Satisfaction registers as an abdominal irritation and the recluse begins salivating. Reaching underneath the table to search for any grease, oils, or dust he can paw into his mouth, he asks "Is this worth the descent?"

Starlight in One's Hand

The joey Zone

LEAH BODINE DRAKE. *The Song of The Sun: Collected Writings*. Edited by David E. Schultz. New York: Hippocampus Press, 2020. 767 pp. $60.00 hc. ISBN: 978-1-61498-266-1. $30.00 tpb. ISBN: 978-1-61498-267-8.

1.

Besides its importance as a publisher of classic weird fiction and its attending scholarship, Hippocampus Press cannot be lauded enough for its fealty to the muse of Verse. Keeping alive the poetry of Clark Ashton Smith, George Sterling, lesser-known lights including Park Barnitz and, even more importantly, contemporary voices such as Donald Sidney-Fryer (long may that troubadour write his songs!) is raison d'être alone for this press. On the horn of the Autumnal Equinox, this collection has finally appeared after being announced three years ago. It is an impressive volume in its physicality, with a two-inch-wide spine and the author's signature in gold on the cloth under the front wraps. What August Derleth and Donald Wandrei did for H. P. Lovecraft's legacy with the publication of *The Outsider and Others* in 1939, David E. Schultz does now for Leah Bodine Drake.

Drake's *A Hornbook for Witches* (1950) was the first collection of poetry published by Arkham House, comprising forty-seven poems. *The Song of The Sun* contains these and the rest of her 360 poems, more than 100 never previously published.

Besides appearing in the small press, in her lifetime Leah Bodine Drake (1904–1964) cracked the market of "the slicks," including the *Saturday Evening Post* and the *New Yorker*. Above and beyond the biggest names in the Arkham House line (Lovecraft, Howard, etc.), she also garnered a positive review upon her first book's release in the *New York Times*. Her 1939 verse "They Run Again" (is there a better lycanthropic ode anywhere?) was quoted in full in the review.

The Song also contains Drake's short stories, two or which originally appeared in *Weird Tales*. The best of these is "Mop-Head" (1951), which was graced with an eldritch illumination by Joseph Eberle sadly not reproduced in this volume. In addition, there are essays and book reviews by her, including "Whimsy and Whamsy" (1949), which—despite Drake's lukewarm assessment—has this reviewer now not only looking for a copy of Stanley Mullen's *Moonfoam and Sorceries* (Gorgon Press), but also for more of the "fan" art of its illustrator, Denver's Roy V. Hunt. Hunt's work proves to be worthy of rediscovery, some of it being unique takes in Lovecraftian art for that time or the present. Thank you, Leah!

There is a lengthy section of Drake's letters, including those to *Weird Tales* (extolling the work of Margaret Brundage, Virgil Finlay, CAS, Algernon Blackwood, and others) and seventy-two to August Derleth alone. Finally, nearly fifty related photographs of Leah Bodine Drake as well as a comprehensive bibliography make this publication even more incredibly useful in re-establishing her importance beyond genre.

2.

Drake is one of the great poets of Faery. Some fine examples of this were published in *A Hornbook* (such as the classic "Changeling"), but one notable early (1933) narrative, "The Ballad of Fair Elspeth," appears here for the first time. The theme of the Pied Piper is used not only in "The Little Piper" (1934) but in "Peddler's Pack." Written in 1939, it was later submitted to Anthony Boucher for the *Magazine of Fantasy and Science Fiction* but rejected. That publication's loss is our gain.

A gnomish peddler offers The Good including

> The missing star
> From the Pleiad's throng;
> The opening bar
> Of the sirens' song

but upon their rejection, leaves only the detritus of The Bad that must be taken:

> A weed from Bluebeard's funeral-wreath,
> Roots of mandrake, dragon's teeth

There's a moral for editors there somewhere!

Another inspiration to Drake is the work of Lord Dunsany. The poem "The Stranger" (1938) and prose "Time and the Sphinx" (1947) are both dedicated to him. The verse "Unhappy Ending" (1935) is the most Dunsanian of all, being a mordant tale similar to "The Hoard of the Gibbelins."

Jason C. Eckhardt adds illustrations, fifteen in number, to the mix. Two fine examples are that for "The Ballad of the Jabberwock" (1946), which concerns the legend (?) of the Jersey Devil, and the one for "The Crows" (1955)—being one of Jason's best works anywhere.

In 1941, Leah wrote in her short essay "To Be a Poet" that "You must *feel* moonlight, *see* the wind, *taste* sunlight and *smell* colour." The best poetry summons visuals with its words. After seeing John Duncan's Symbolist painting of 1923, *Ivory, Apes and Peacocks,* Drake wrote "The Journey of the Queen of Sheba" in 1937. Originally slated as the finale of *A Hornbook for Witches,* it was cut due to length as well as being deemed only "borderline fantastical" by the writer and by her editor Derleth. May we be able to tarry near *these* borders longer—it is the standout piece in this collection.

> She sat in a peacock-shade throne
> On a grey beast out of myth, whose walk
> Woke the thunder beneath the ground,
> And whose tusks were inlaid with orichalch.

Coming down

> From slopes of the Mountains of the Moon
> Where rivers are born and dragons hiss;
> Plumes of ostrich, and ivory horns
> Heaped with spices and ambergris.

Bejeweled verse such as this could have suitably adorned any one of Lin Carter's anthologies for the Ballantine Adult Fantasy Series back in the day.

3.

> It is necessary for a poet to be steeped in some great tradition of mysticism.
>
> —John Livingston Lowes

Lowes was a Harvard professor whose seminal work was *The Road to Xanadu* (1927), an examination of S. T. Coleridge's sources (and one of this reviewer's most treasured volumes on the shelf). This quotation was appended to Drake's essay "A Poem Should Have" in one of her personal scrapbooks. By her own *rite,* Leah Bodine Drake's entire oeuvre is part of this great tradition, woven into the tapestry of imagination.

I respectfully take exception to her own evaluation of her work, however. In "Minor Poet" (1947) Drake relates that

> On mornings when no withered leaf
> Rattled a branch, I've watched the strange
> Dance of the lonely hippogriff,
> Wings folded—still beyond the range
>
> Of my crude weapon!

For someone who had enjoyed popular reception of her art during her life, Leah Bodine Drake still wanted more. Her "heart fully aware of the legacy of myth" (Schultz) that makes us who we are was her greatest crude weapon. For fantasy readers, this collection is as good a gateway to poetry as any. The magick of her art is accessible as starlight reflected in dew drops on that withered leaf held in one's hand.

Nodens in the Nutmeg State

Edward Guimont

SAM GAFFORD. *The House of Nodens*. Portland, OR: Dark Regions Press, 2017. 252 pp. $22.00 tpb. ISBN: 978-1-7274-9054-1.

In 1975, Bill Simmons is a typical thirteen-year-old geek. He hangs out with his friends Mike Dolan, Ryan Bloom, and Tim Skerrit; begins to date his first girlfriend Tina Kidd; reads comic books, Edgar Rice Burroughs, and even H. P. Lovecraft—and explores the woods around his hometown of New Milford, Connecticut. On one such excursion, the boys come across the titular house of Nodens, a circle of worship for an ancient malevolent deity—and whose veneration the boys resume, with deadly consequences. Forty years later, Bill is an alcoholic, friendless divorcee living in Bridgeport, whose memories of Nodens begin to resume just as a serial killer called "The Deer Hunter," who leaves the remains of his women victims arranged in elaborate tableaus, returns to activity. The story of just what happened in 1975, and how it relates to the events of 2015, is revealed by cutting between each time frame, the activities of the past and present building towards a parallel climax.

You could be excused if the description of the late Sam Gafford's debut novel sounds familiar. There are clear similarities not only to Stephen King's 1986 *It*—although Robert M. Price, in the only other published review of the novel, instead suggested it drew more from King's pre-*It* works (Price 37)—but also the 2013–15 NBC TV adaptation of *Hannibal* and the 2014 first season of HBO's *True Detective*. However, this is not to accuse Gafford of plagiarizing King, Bryan Fuller, or Nic Pizzolatto, but rather to demonstrate that he draws from the same common pool of themes and influences that they do. Indeed, this is apparent from the fact that *Nodens* has some preemptive similarities to the 2019 third season of *True Detec-*

tive.

Gafford's choice of Nodens as a villain is an interesting one. As Marco Frenschkowski noted, Nodens is unique; beyond its exceedingly rare appearance in the Mythos, Nodens stands out as one of Lovecraft's few benevolent deities, as well as one of the only ones he used that was not only not of his own creation, but actually worshipped in history (*CF* 2.213; Frenschkowski 3–4; Gafford 144). The benevolence of Lovecraft's Nodens is completely absent in Gafford's version. However, the key may be found in Frenschkowski's observation that Lovecraft seemed to use Nodens as an avatar of a wistful attraction to the past—something that is fully compatible with the lonely older Bill's obsession toward his lost love, Tina (Frenschkowski 7; Gafford 179–80).

The use of such an obscure Mythos deity by Gafford is also congruent with his generally subtle usage of direct Lovecraft references. Price in his review does claim that "No other Mythos names are mentioned, which is good. We all know how deadly clichés can be in would-be Lovecraftian tales" (Price 37). While I agree with his second sentence, his first is in fact wrong—perhaps a testament to just how subtle Gafford was. The forest circle where Nodens' shrine is located is referred to as the "blasted heath," a reference to the Gardner farm from "The Colour out of Space"—whose description, S. T. Joshi has noted, was based on the Devil's Hopyard of nearby East Haddam, Connecticut (Gafford 63; *CF* 2.368; Joshi 412n17). Mike forces his friends to worship Nodens by "making the Voorish sign or making the marks of the dholes upon our bodies" (Gafford 190), respectively referring to "The Dunwich Horror" (*CF* 2.450) and *The Dream-Quest of Unknown Kadath,* the same source as Nodens (*CF* 2.132). The prayer to summon Nodens is the Magna Mater incantation from "The Rats in the Walls" (Gafford 230; *CF* 1.396). Two of the last words in the novel are even "cool air" (Gafford 249).

But these are still largely superficial callbacks to Lovecraft's writing, and the true subtlety of Gafford's use of the Mythos as a setting is his ability to draw in elements from beyond the Old Gentleman. The description of the "blasted heath" seems to draw not only from the stone circles of Ithaqua worship established by August Derleth, but the specific one located in coastal Connecticut from the story "Jendick's Swamp" by Bridgeport native Joseph Payne Brennan (Gafford 63; Derleth 72; Brennan 190–92, 198). Adult Bill's estranged son, Gary, is mentioned as living in Wisconsin; this has to be Gafford inverting the relationship of Lovecraft's friend Maurice Moe, a Wisconsin native whose son Robert moved to Bridgeport (Gafford 225; *SL* 5.177). And indeed, the heavy focus on Bridgeport—chapter 32 of the novel is an extended overview of the city's geography and history on par with Lovecraft's attention to Providence in *The Case of Charles Dexter Ward*—is even more apt given Michael J. Bielawa's recent work illustrating how 1880s medical experiments in the city clearly influenced "Herbert West—Reanimator" (Gafford 193–200; Bielawa 38–51).

The attention to Bridgeport in particular reflects what to me personally was a major appeal of the novel: the fact that, unlike the sparse earlier efforts like "Jendick's Swamp," *The House of Nodens* is the first full-on Mythos story to use Connecticut as a setting—not only Connecticut geography (which it certainly does), but its history and folklore as well. The novel establishes that not only was Connecticut's most famous ghost town, Dudleytown, linked to the ancient worship of Nodens, but the entity caused the famous 1918 case of Harriet Bank Clarke's demon-sighting and suicide there (Gafford 18, 61 211, 231; Gencarella 190–98). Gafford also draws from darker, more contemporary Connecticut myths. Paralleling the misadventures of modern-day Bill, the novel follows a group of state police and FBI agents tracking the Deer Hunter and associated claims of pedophilia and cover-ups. The climax of the novel reveals that the state police are part of a conspiracy, "a cabal . . . all high-ranking, power people. They're the ones who decide everything." This "cabal" protected the Deer Hunter, whose killings were rituals aimed at Nodens, whom the cabal also worships (Gafford 236–38). The term "cabal" in association with a group of demonic pedophiles embedded in government bureaucracy might bring to mind national conspiracy theories of recent years, such as Pizzagate and QAnon. However, it made me think of the claims promoted by local fringe political figures, such as Lee Whitnum and Minnie Gonzalez, whose claims of a conspiracy of homosexual pedophile Jews using the state judiciary to destroy traditional families has done concrete damage to Connecticut's LGBT population over the past decade (Dubois).

While an interesting way to merge both contemporary Connecticut political and folkloric legends into the Cthulhu Mythos framework, the Nodens cabal is also an illustration of some of the less effective aspects of *The House of Nodens,* as the conspiracy's true nature, goals, and ultimate purpose and extent are never resolved in the novel—indeed, the conspiracy is introduced within the last twenty pages. The non-linear storyline of the novel, and the broken psyche of alcoholic, hallucinating adult Bill also present a number of narrative potentials that are never fully capitalized on. At several points in the novel, I wondered if the reader was supposed to be led to think that Bill could possibly actually be the Deer Hunter—but the writing never seems to introduce this idea fully, leaving me to wonder if I was imagining that to be Gafford's intent or not. In his review, Price states that novel features deep characterization guided by Gafford's "wise insights into genuine human beings and their psychology" (Price 37). While I might not commit entirely into the depth of the characterization, especially for the brief viewpoints we get of characters other than Bill, Bill himself was very well portrayed, especially for a debut novel where the same character has to be depicted across hundreds of pages as both a teenager and an adult. The character development is in the upper tier of Mythos authors and Lovecraft pastiches, and with respect to Lovecraft, far beyond anything the Old Gentleman was capable of developing. As so much of the novel is seen through the eyes of either teen or adult Bill, being portrayed through the view of the world shaped by his own neuroses and disabilities, that the success of the novel is a testament to Gafford's ability to develop his main character effectively.

And despite the above critiques, *The House of Nodens* is a success, in three ways. First and most importantly, it is a success as a horror novel; it stands on its own, and someone with no knowledge of Lovecraft can enjoy it fully. This flows from the second aspect of its success: it is the sort of Cthulhu Mythos story that we need, the kind less like the pastiches of Derleth or Lin Carter and more like those of Caitlín R. Kiernan, where the emphasis is less on recycling stock terms like squamous, eldritch, or Yog-Sothoth, and more on developing the emotions of dread and alienation at the heart of the most effective works of Lovecraftian fiction. The third aspect of its success is that this is the first major foray of a Cthulhu Mythos novel into Connecticut, a welcome integration of a neglected New England state and its rich folklore into one of the most quintessentially Yankee corpus of lore and legend of the past century.

I only met Sam Gafford once, when he and Jason C. Eckhardt presented their graphic novel *Some Notes on a Non-Entity* at Lovecraft Arts & Sciences in Providence on the fateful date of 15 March 2018, the eighty-first anniversary of Lovecraft's death. Gafford himself died on 20 July 2019. At the time, I had not yet read *The House of Nodens,* which I regret; if I had, I without a doubt would have spoken with him at length on it and his sources of inspiration. As it is, I am glad that even in some small fashion I can help continue to spread the awareness of Gafford and his work after death, and help keep his legacy alive in that way.

Works Cited

Bielawa, Michael J. *Wicked Bridgeport*. Charleston, SC: History Press, 2012.

Brennan, Joseph Payne. "Jendick's Swamp." 1987. In Robert M. Price, ed. *The Ithaqua Cycle: The Wind-Walker of the Icy Wastes: 14 Tales*. Hayward, CA: Chaosium, 1997. 188–99.

Derleth, August. "The Snow-Thing." 1941. In Robert M. Price, ed. *The Ithaqua Cycle: The Wind-Walker of the Icy Wastes: 14 Tales*. Hayward, CA: Chaosium, 1997. 69–79.

Dubois, Mark L. "Extorting the Tyranny of the Majority?" *Yahoo! Finance* (20 June 2018). finance.yahoo.com/news/extorting-tyranny-majority-125337490.html

Frenschkowski, Marco. "Nodens—Metamorphosis of a Deity." *Crypt of Cthulhu* No. 108 (1994): 3–8, 18.

Gencarella, Stephen. *Spooky Trails and Tall Tales Connecticut: Hiking the State's Legends, Hauntings, and History*. Guilford, CT: Falcon, 2019.

Joshi, S. T. "Explanatory Notes." In H. P. Lovecraft. *The Thing on the Doorstep and Other Weird Stories,* Ed. S. T. Joshi. New York: Penguin, 2001. 367–443.

Lovecraft, H. P. *The Dream-Quest of Unknown Kadath*. In *Collected Fiction: 1926–1930* [CF]. New York: Hippocampus Press, 2017.

Price, Robert M. "Review: *The House of Nodens* by Sam Gafford." *Crypt of Cthulhu* No. 108 (2017): 37.

Sandalwood and Jade: The Weird and Fantastic Verse of Lin Carter

Leigh Blackmore

> A Poet sees the beauty in the common things of life:
> The wonder in an evening star, or in the tempest's strife;
> The magic in a flower, and the music in a stream;
> The glory in a vision and the splendor in a dream."
> —Lin Carter

Lin(wood) Vrooman Carter was born in St. Petersburg, Florida, on 9 June 1930. He died 7 February 1988, aged only fifty-seven, after a long and prolific career as writer and editor in the fantasy and horror fields. During much of his writing career he lived in Hollis, New York.

In the late 1940s, beginning as a teenage fan, he first appeared on the sf/fantasy scene, contributing many entertaining letters of comment to such magazines as *Startling Stories, Thrilling Wonder Stories, Planet Stories,* and *Famous Fantastic Mysteries*. He began to contribute interior art to fanzines, and to write and publish his own short fiction.

In this essay, I provide a mere overview of Carter's poetic oeuvre. One of the difficulties in assessing his complete poetic works is the difficult in obtaining some of the limited-edition chapbooks in which his verse was collected.

In his "Author's Note" to the collection *Dreams from R'lyeh,* Carter states:

> Like many another novelist and story-teller to the manner born, my first ambition was in the direction of poetry. As most of my colleagues eventually found to their chagrin, the direction was a false lead, beckoning into a blind labyrinth. But beginning about 1948, verses by the countless hundreds literally poured from my brain . . . (71)

Whether Carter is to be believed about having composed poems "by the countless hundreds" is dubious. If it is true, he must have destroyed many, many verses from his pen, for his poetic oeuvre overall is small. He also states that "from many thousands [of poems], I have culled a rigorous few" (72). It is doubtful that Carter wrote as many as a thousand poems, let alone several thousand, but more research among Carter's papers at the David M. Rubenstein Rare Book Manuscript Library, Duke University Libraries (see archives.lib.duke.edu/catalog/carterlin) may reveal some previously unpublished verses.

He goes on write: "It goes without saying that by far the greatest portion of these 'poems' were the purest essence of vapid doggerel—puerile and derivative, stale and juiceless—mere juvenile garbage . . . I strove for unthinkable goals: to be a *real* poet." One of his poems, he tells us, was an *Alexandriad,* some five thousand lines of iambic pentameter on the theme of a certain Macedonian conqueror. But he "set [it] aside."

He tells us that the earliest of the verses in the volume is "Shard," "written about 1947 when I was a boy of seventeen mooning away over books in sunny St. Petersburg, Florida." This poem was first printed in *Loki* No. 1 (Spring 1948) and was collected in Carter's first slim book of verse, *Sandalwood and Jade*.

Carter's first *published* poem appears to have been "Shadow Song," in *Kotan* 1, No. 1 (September 1948). Hot on its heels came "Shard," and then "The Song of Liane the Dreamer," which appeared in *Scientifantasy* No. 2 (Winter 1949). Another poem, "Kooribal," was published in *Scientifantasy* No. 4 (September 1949). *Scientifantasy* was edited by Bill Kroll and John Grossman and ran only four issues, through 1948–49. Carter published one poem in 1950, "The Lotus Eater," *Fanscient* No. 12 (Summer 1950), edited by Donald M. Day, and one in 1951, "The Walker on the Wind," *Asmodeus* No. 2 (Fall 1951), edited by Alan H. Pesetsky and Michael deAngelis of Gargoyle Press. On an interesting side note here for Lovecraftians, the rather mysterious deAngelis had previously published a review of Lovecraft's *Something about Cats and Other Pieces* (1949) (*Gargoyle* 1, No. 1, 1950) and also published an article on Lovecraft in the same issue as Carter's "The Walker on the Wind," titled "H. P. Lovecraft: A Revaluation." *Asmodeus* No. 3 (Spring 1952) featured Carter's sixth published poem, "Once in Fabled Grandeur."

Carter's first book was the slim 24-page chapbook *Sandalwood and Jade: Poems of the Exotic and Strange* (1951), published when he was twenty-one years of age. The main title irresistibly recalls Clark Ashton Smith's similarly titled poetry volumes *Ebony and Crystal* (1922) and *Sandalwood* (1925). *Sandalwood and Jade* was published under Carter's own imprint, The Sign of the Centaur. The publisher, based in St. Petersburg, Florida, was, of course, Carter himself, and he also provided the cover illustration. Published in an edition of only 100 signed copies, *Sandalwood and Jade*, containing thirty poems, is now an incredibly rare pamphlet, worth between $200 and $500. Technically, *Sandalwood and Jade* is Carter's first book.

Eleven of the poems here had been published previously, two of them in two different magazines. These were "The Walker on the Wind," *St. Petersburg Times* (April 1948), winner of the '48 Elizabeth Buchtenkirk Award; "Mars," *Spaceteer* No. 2 (March–April 1948); "Nightwind," *Triton* No. 4 (1949), winner of a '48 St. Petersburg Poetry League Award; "Pan," *Dream Quest* No. 6 (July 1948); "The Golden City," *Loki* No. 1 (Spring 1948), *Palmetto and Pine Literary Supplement* No. 2 (1948), winner of a St. Petersburg Poetry League Award, 1948; "The Fantast," *Gorgon* 2, No. 3 (March 1949); "Shard," *Loki* No. 1 (Spring 1948), *Palmetto and Pine Literary Supplement* No. 1 (1947); "The Song of Laine the Dreamer," *Scientifantasy* No. 2 (Winter 1949); "The Wizard Isle," *Challenge* No. 1 (Summer 1950); "Kooribaal," *Scientifantasy* No. 4 (Summer 1949); "The Lotus-Eater," *Fanscient* No. 12 (Summer 1950); "Song of the Sorcerer" *Challenge* No. 2 (Fall 1950). The other poems in this collection were previously unpublished.

Palmetto and Pine was the school newspaper of Carter's school, the St. Petersburg High School. He was in several clubs at the school, including poetry and art clubs. (See gndn.wordpress.com/2017/02/07/lin-carter-class-of-48/ for some high school photos of Carter.) I have been unable to source any information on the St. Petersburg Poetry League; it may have been one of Carter's high school clubs, or a small group of poetry devotees that met locally in St. Petersburg. Likewise, I have been unable to trace information about the Elizabeth Buchtenkirk Award. However, the fact that at least three of Carter's early poems won awards speaks highly of his nascent talent in this field.

Sandalwood and Jade is omitted from the database of Carter's work on ISFDB.com. Fortunately, I have had access to a scan of its complete contents. The poems included are: "Couplet," "Pirate Gold," "The Star-Gazer," "The Night Kings," "Mars," "The Arabian Nights," "Beyond the Gates of Dream," "The Wizard Isle," "Of the Princess Liu-Shang," "The Gods Looked Down," "The Lotus-Eater," "The Splendor in a Dream," 'The Fantast," "To Lord Dunsany," "Pan," "Shard," "Walker on the Wind," "Nightwind," "When Solomon Was King," "The Jungle-Song," "Babylon," "The Song of Laine the Dreamer," "Kooribaal," "To a Chinese Maiden," "The Book of Djinns," "Once in Fabled Grandeur," "Wanderlust," "In an Oriental Twilight," "Song of the Sorcerer," and "The Golden City." Each poem's title is lettered by Carter, with an accompanying illustration by him.

The poems of this collection are a mix of formal rhyming verse and free verse. Let us quote the lovely "Song of Laine the Dreamer" as but one example from this volume:

> My dreams are works of golden wizardry
> Of dawnstar glow and song of siren wrought,
> And twenty thousand shards of memory
>
> Of sweeter worlds exalted, clad in light,
> Wherein the myriad fancies of my mind
> Take form and shape and substance from the night,
>
> Wherein I stand a God, enthroned in lands
> Where moons of misty opal lift the dark
> And crystal cities glimmer in the sands.
>
> Where nightingales in moonlit gardens sing,
> Where lamps of beaten bronze allay the dusk
> And androsphinxes soar on leathern wing.

In his foreword to *Sandalwood and Jade,* Carter reveals many of the early influences upon his poetic work. He states he has written poetry for six years, which indicates he began to write poetry around 1946. Oddly, he references a poem called "Canal," which he says was "the first of them printed anywhere"—apparently in the September 1947 issue of Beak Taylor's *Canadian Fandom*. But this poem does not appear in the book! Joseph "Beak" Taylor was an early Toronto fan and founder of the Derelicts (Toronto SF Society).

Carter cites Robert E. Howard and C. A. Smith as his favorite fantasy poets. His favorites among the non-fantasy poets are given as

> England's Milton, Shelley ("Ode to the West Wind"), Keats, Coleridge ("Kubla Khan"), Oscar Wilde (especially "The Sphinx"), the classic Chinese poets Li Po, Tu Fu, Fo Chu-I ("The Island of Pines"), the Persian poet Hafiz in the LeGallienne translation, the incomparable *Rubaiyat of Omar Khayyam,* and the great love-poem *Black Marigolds* of the Sanskrit poet Chauraz (translated from the *Chauraspenchasi*ka by Powys Mathers), as well as France's Baudelaire, America's Poe, and the popular American poet Don Blanding ("Vagabond's House").

Following publication of *Sandalwood and Jade,* Carter served for two years in the United States Army (Infantry, Korea, 1951–53). A letter he published in *Startling Stories* (March 1953) reveals his rank as corporal.

Following army service and now aged twenty-three, Carter attended Columbia University (1953–54), during which time he attended Leonie Adams's Poetry Workshop. He was a copywriter for some years before writing full-time. During his first year at Columbia, he issued *Galleon of Dream: Poems of Fantasy and Wonder* (St. Petersburg, FL: The Sign of the Centaur, 1953). This second 24-page companion volume of his poetry (in an edition of 200 signed copies) collected ten items of previously published verse from 1948 to 1953 in various fanzines and little magazines including *The Time Machine, Loki, Palmetto and Pine, Poemzine, Sky Hook, Mezrab, Cataclysm,* and *Starlanes,* plus a further twenty-one poems previously unpublished. Again, Carter himself provided the cover illustration and some interior artwork. *Galleon of Dream* saw Carter hit his stride as a poet. The volume was dedicated to Doris Margaret Derrick, "friend and teacher." Since there were 200 copies of this pamphlet printed, it is, though scarce, not as rare as *Sandalwood and Jade;* copies can be obtained from out-of-print dealers for between $30 to $60. There is also a print-on-demand reprint of *Galleon of Dream* available from Literary Licensing LLC.

In the foreword to the booklet, Carter writes:

> I do not claim to be an innovator. In fact, I fear my verse is stuffily conventional in form. I prefer lyrical poetry to any or all of the confusing, uneven and unreadable verse—forms in which modern poetry is torturing it's [*sic*] public. My idols are the poets like Shelley, Tennyson, Masefield, Byron, the unknown or unremembered author of the "Kasidah of Hadji Abdu el Yezdi," Spenser ("Faery Queen"), the Sanskrit poet Bilhana, the contemporary lyric poet George Sterling, Lilith Lorraine, and certain bits from Kipling and Stevenson—although these gentlemen [*sic*] were far better as novelists than as versifiers.

Some of these references indicate Carter's extensive reading of verse not commonly known in the West. For instance, the *Kasidah* is a long English-language poem written by "Hâjî Abdû El-Yezdî," actually a pseudonym of Sir Richard Francis Burton (1821–1890), the well-known Arabist and explorer. Burton claimed to be the "translator" of the poem, to which he gives the English title "Lay of the Higher Law." It is thus a pseudo-translation, purporting to be based on an original, nonexistent Persian text. The *Kasidah* is a distillation of Sufi thought in the poetic idiom of that mystical tradition. Bilhana, a Sanskrit poet of many centuries ago (scholars disagree as to the exact identity and time-period of the poet), is known for the *Caurapañcāśikā* (*The Love Thief*), a Sanskrit love poem in fifty stanzas, tells of a thief's secret love for a princess. That Carter, at the tender age of twenty-three, could cite such poets as an influence indicates his deep interest in literature of cultures other than the received Western Canon.

Carter later altered his view of poetic form, as noted by L. Sprague de Camp in his introduction to Carter's only professionally published volume of verse, *Dreams from R'lyeh* (1975). By the time of this book's publication, Carter was more enamored of free verse than of formalist poetry, citing Ezra Pound, whose opinion was that "all those limitations of rhyme and metre just get in the way. Throw 'em out!" ([xi]).

Galleon of Dream contains the following poems: "Galleon of Dream," "Nightmare," "Dark Elixer [*sic*]," "Changeling," "Futility," "If I Were King of Kooribaal," "In the Days of King Arthur," "Golden Fleece," "Fiddler's Green," "Hashish and Sandalwood," "Magic Carpet," "Wish," "Beside the Shalimar," "Shadow-Song," "Cathay," "Treasure Island," "Storybook Seas," "The Yellow-Brick Road to Oz," "Fairyland," "City in the Sea," "Nocturne," "Vagabond's Song," "Oft Have Visited Eastern Lands," "Collectors Corner," "Ivanhoe," "Song of the Crusades," "The Wind in the Rigging," "Tradewinds," "The Star-Storm," and "The Horns of Elfland."

From the titles of the poems alone, one can gather a sense of Carter's thematic preoccupations: exotic locales of history, mythology and legend, and verse based on stores of heroic valor.

"Galleon of Dream," the collection's title poem, is a four-stanza poem rhyming ababcc. It is pure fantasy, dealing with the poet dreaming of exotic cities and realms such as Samarkand, Zanzibar, Turkistan, Trebizond, Araby, Cathay, and Kurdistan, and glimpsing gryphons, mermaids, and other fabulous creatures:

> But when morning gilds the sky
> I moor my Galleon on high
> And forsake the briny deep
> And the golden realms of sleep:
> I must wake to face the day,
> With only dreams of my Cathay.

"Nightmare" is told in blank verse. The poet is here caught up by a "thunder-winged Chimera"—a "creature black as Satan's wing" (rather reminiscent of Lovecraft's night-gaunts) that "flew with me above the dazzling suns." After encountering various nightmare monsters including "flame-winged Demogorgons," the Chimera and the poet encounter a vast snaky head, "the head all crawling with a thousand coils"—a vast, coiled shape "whose lashless lids blazed like twin gulfs of hellish fire, / A gaping maw thick-set with javelined fangs / That oozed a lethal saliva; a maw that might devour at one gulp a sun." The thing has "tremendous wings like ebon continents / That dwarf the very pillars of the night." The two monstrous creatures battle, and the Chimera drops the poet who falls through shrieking chaos . . . The subject matter and some of the language of this poem are highly reminiscent of Clark Ashton Smith's epic *The Hashish-Eater*.

"Dark Elixer" is a 12-line poem in couplets, a rhyming chant like a witches' invocation listing the ingredients that go into the elixir.

"Changeling" is again in blank verse and relates how the poet feels called by the coldly shining stars "from this drab life up to wonders, / And to glories that I seem to have known before / As if from some previous life." This hint of reincarnation recalls Smith, and also perhaps the end of Lovecraft's "The Shadow over Innsmouth."

"Futility," another blank-verse poem, addresses what the poet sees as the futility of human existence, since we can never understand the cosmos or life in all its variety.

The description and assessment of other poems in this collection must await a fuller examination of Carter's verse than this overview.

In April–June 1959, aged twenty-nine, Carter wrote the non-fantastic *A Letter to Judith: A Work of Poetry*. He issued this from New York City on 29 June 1959 in an edition of 500 copies "for private distribution to friends of the author and his wife," i.e., his first wife, Judith Ellen Hershkovitz, whom he married in 1959 but divorced in 1960.

A Letter to Judith is a single poem in a pamphlet of 16 pages, again self-published, though with no stated imprint as on the earlier poetry volumes. While very scarce, unsigned copies of this little booklet can be had on the secondhand market for $30 or less. Carter appears to have signed several copies. One known is signed in green ink. Another known signed copy is that inscribed to August Derleth, publisher of Arkham House; the inscription reads: "To August Derleth with all best wishes and regards, Lin Carter May, 1960." **Signed** copies of *A Letter to Judith* are extremely rare and can sell for around $500.

The inside front cover of the booklet lists several collections of poetry as forthcoming. These are: *The Adorations,* a cycle of sonnets in five "decades"; *Fantasmagoria,* a dream; and *Dreams from R'lyeh,* a sonnet-sequence. *Dreams from R'lyeh* would ultimately be issued by Arkham House in 1975; however, I am unsure if these other projected volumes were completed or even begun. They were certainly not issued.

Following *Galleon of Dreams,* if one discounts the non-fantastic *A Letter to Judith,* there was then a poetic hiatus of around eight years until August Derleth selected five poems by Carter for inclusion in his anthology *Fire and Sleet and Candlelight* (1961). These poems were "Lunae Custodiens," "The Dream-Daemon," "The Sabbat," "Carcosa," and "Dark Yuggoth." "Lunae Custodiens" was collected in the general section of the volume *Dreams from R'lyeh,* while the other four poems were incorporated into the actual *Dreams from R'lyeh: A Sonnet Sequence,* numbered as follows: "XIX. The Sabbat," "XXII. Carcosa," "XXIV. The Dream-Daemon," and "XXV. Dark Yuggoth."

In 1963, Carter married Noel Vreeland when they both worked for Prentice-Hall publishers; they divorced in 1975.

We have seen that the sonnet-sequence *Dreams from R'lyeh* was conceived as early as 1959. Most of the poems for it were composed in the 1960s. Between 1964 and 1968, Carter published another twenty-nine Lovecraftian sonnets in the pages of *Amra,* the sword and sorcery devotee's magazine edited by George H. Scithers. The following issues contained seven of these poems, which at that time were not sequenced as they would later be in *Dreams from R'lyeh:* 2, No. 28 (June 1964), 2, No. 32 (March 1965), and 2, No. 46 (April 1968). *Amra* 2, No. 47 (August 1968) contained eight Lovecraftian sonnets. From this, we can see that most of the poems in the *Dreams from R'lyeh* sonnet sequence were composed around a decade before their eventual collection in the Arkham House volume. *Amra* 2, No. 46 (April 1968) also featured a section of "Limericks Barsoomian" by various authors, including one by Carter.

In 1966, Carter had published his first novel, a standalone called *The Star Magicians*. Throughout the late 1960s, he published several more novels in tandem with other writers, which were published in the then-popular back-to-back format. Carter's *The Thief of Thoth* even appeared back-to-back in 1968 with Lovecraft Circle writer Frank Belknap Long's *And Others Shall Be Born*. By now he was publishing novels prolifically, including his *Thongor* series (1965–70), his *Thoth* series (1968–69), his *Green Star Rises* series (1972–74), his *Great Imperium* series (1966–71), and the mid-late 1960s "completions" (with L. Sprague de Camp) of various works by Robert E. Howard, including previously unfinished Conan and Kull of Valusia stories. From 1969 onward, Carter was a freelance writer and editorial consultant. The Thongor novels often include epigraphs to chapters—fragments of poetry that purport to be extracts from longer, epic works. They are mainly in the vein of Robert E. Howard's poetic work.

Carter published more poetry sporadically during the 1970s. "To Clark Ashton Smith" and "All Hallows' Eve" appeared in August Derleth's magazine, the *Arkham Collector* (Winter and Summer 1970 issues respectively). "The Forgotten" was in *Witchcraft and Sorcery* No. 5 (January–February 1971). "Black Thirst," which would ultimately be numbered IX and included in the *Dreams from R'lyeh* sonnet sequence, appeared in the *Arkham Collector* for Winter 1971. Carter included the poem "The Descent of Ishtar to the Netherworld" in his own anthology *Golden Cities, Far* (Ballantine Books, 1970) and "Litany to Hastur" in his anthology of Cthulhu Mythos material, *The Spawn of Cthulhu* (Ballantine Books, 1971). "Death Song of Conan the Cimmerian" appeared in the *Howard Collector* No. 17 (Autumn 1972). Several of these original poems saw reprinting in *Dreams from R'lyeh,* which also gathered many of (though not all) his previously published verses written between 1964–68.

Dreams from R'lyeh appeared in an edition of 3000 copies (according to the book's colophon, although Sheldon Jaffrey's

Arkham House Companion states 3152 copies were printed, as does S. T. Joshi in his *Sixty Years of Arkham House*). L. Sprague de Camp provided the volume's foreword, "Merlin on the Queens Express." The book is a slim volume of 72 pages, containing the thirty-one poems of the actual sonnet cycle *Dreams from R'lyeh,* together with another fifteen poems, for a total of forty-six poems. The poems in the "Other Poems" section of the volume are "Lunae Custodiens," "Merlin, Enchanted," "To Clark Ashton Smith," "Once in Fabled Grandeur," "The Night Kings," "All Hallows' Eve," "Shard" (Carter's earliest acknowledged poem), "The Wind in the Rigging," "Diombar's Song of the Last Battle," "The Elf-King's Castle," "To Lord Dunsany," "The Forgotten," "Golden Age," "Lines Written to a Painting by Hannes Bok," and "Death-Song of Conan the Cimmerian."

Leon Neilson's *Arkham House Books: A Collector's Guide* assigns it a value of $50 in dust jacket. However, there are plenty of copies to be found on the Internet for between $25 and $35. Although the book is rarely encountered signed, there are two signed copies for sale on Abebooks.com as I write, one at $100 and the other at $250.

S. T. Joshi (*Sixty Years of Arkham House* 136) refers to *Dreams from R'lyeh* as "the collected poetry of Carter," but this is not entirely accurate. According to the book's dust jacket blurb, the volume collects together "all of the macabre verse of Lin Carter that he considers worthy of preservation."

Dreams from R'lyeh: A Sonnet Cycle is a sequence of weird poems clearly inspired by Lovecraft's famous sonnet cycle *Fungi from Yuggoth*. The individual poems were all written between 1961 and 1971. (For the dates of composition of individual poems, see ISFDB www.isfdb.org/cgi-bin/ea.cgi?353.)

In macabre verse, the sonnet cycle tells a loose story whereby the narrator, a youth named Wilbur Nathaniel Hoag, discovers some tomes of eldritch knowledge, which discovery leads him to investigate dark deities who inhabit weird worlds, and the depraved followers of these deities who assist them, as in Lovecraft's Cthulhu Mythos tales, in bringing forth chaos and destruction to the earth and humankind.

The book contains the following poems: *Dreams from*

R'lyeh: A Sonnet Cycle [umbrella title]: "I. Remembrances"; "II. Arkham"; "III. The Festival"; "IV. The Old Wood"; "V. The Locked Attic"; "V. The Shunned Church"; "VII. The Last Ritual"; "VIII. The Library"; "IX. Black Thirst"; "X. The Elder Age"; "XI. Lost R'lyeh"; "XII. Unknown Kadath"; "XIII. Abdul Alhazred"; "XIV. Hyperborea"; "XV. The Book of Eibon"; "XVI. Tsathoggua"; "XVII. Black Zimbabwe"; "XVIII. The Return"; "XIX. The Sabbat"; "XX. Black Lotus"; "XXI. The Unspeakable"; "XXII. Carcosa"; "XXIII. The Candidate"; "XXIV. The Dream-Demon"; "XXV. Dark Yuggoth"; "XXVI. The Silver Key"; "XXVII. The Peaks Beyond Throk"; "XXVIII. Spawn of the Black Goat"; "XXIX. Beyond"; "XXX. The Accursed"; and "XXXI. The Million Favored Ones."

Hoag, an inhabitant of Arkham and the last of his line, apparently disappeared and was presumed dead. Hoag was also related to Obed Marsh of the dreaded Innsmouth Marshes. The poems in the collection are the only clue to Hoag's ultimate fate; the originals are housed in the Miskatonic University Library.

H. P. Lovecraft once lamented his self-perceived lack of originality thus: "There are my Poe pieces, and my Dunsany pieces, but alas! where are any Lovecraft pieces?" Carter, however, never wrote: "There are my E. R. Burroughs pieces and my Clark Ashton Smith pieces and my Howard pieces, but alas! where are any Carter pieces?" An unabashed lifelong fan, he was happy to spend his writing career paying homage to those writers whose work in the fantasy field thrilled and delighted him. For Carter, pastiche was a high form of tribute. The thirty-one-sonnet *Dreams from R'lyeh* sequence (though not the other poems from *Dreams from R'lyeh*) was reprinted as part of Robert M. Price's collection of Carter's work *The Xothic Legend Cycle: The Complete Mythos Fiction of Lin Carter* (1997).

I have traced three contemporary reviews of *Dreams from R'lyeh*, as follows: J. Goldfrank in *WSFA Journal*, 85 (August 1975): R29–R30; W. McPherson in *Science Fiction Review Monthly* 3 (May 1975): [20–21]; and Fritz Leiber in *Fantastic Stories* 25, No. 3 (May 1976): 116–17. Unfortunately, I have not had access to copies of these reviews to see how the volume was critically received at the time of publication.

A much later review was written by one "C. D. Whateley" (pen-name of Charles Lovecraft, himself a weird poet and the proprietor of P'rea Press, a publisher of fantastical verse) for *Crypt of Cthulhu* No. 13 (Roodmas 1983): 47. An effusive yet poetically beautiful and enthusiastic review by a lifelong fan of Lovecraft and the weird, Whateley writes:

> Quite simply, *Dreams from R'lyeh* is a totally, masterfully and uncompromisingly fabulous enthralling volume comprising forty-six magical poems of varying length, which demand to be read and acclaimed. In every star-borne and intensive page it rings with the phantasy bell of a true and prolific dreamer's phantasmal subtleties of colour and happiness in exquisite poems of fantasy, or freezing the blood with a connected series of Cthulhoid terrors, each with its own impactive shudder, and eventually reeling off like a strain of demented music into macro-depths of interstellar horror and poisonous nightmare . . . [The sequence invokes] odious partnership to the "Fungi from Yuggoth" sonnet cycle, but further gives full rein to a glorious fantaisical steed of his own, whose hoofs touch up gleams and rain and stardust in a lovely halter of gorgeous expression, giving to Fantasy a marvellous brooch of elder wonder to emphasises her already beautiful robe."

Surely the highest praise of Carter's verse ever penned!

Carter continued as a prolific novelist with his *Chronicles of Kylix* (1971–84), the *Callisto* series (1972–78), his *Gondwane Epic* (1969–78), *The Mysteries of Mars* series (1973–84), the *Zarkon* series (1975–87), the *Zanthodon* series (1979–82), and the *Terra Magica* series (1982–88), as well as numerous singleton novels and some collections.

Carter's poetic output dropped dramatically (and probably quite understandably, in view of his prolific novel writing) after the publication of *Dreams from R'lyeh*.

Carter wrote two poetry series during the 1980s. The first was *Limericks from Yuggoth* (umbrella title), consisting of four separate limerick "cycles." The first gathering of these humorous Lovecraftian verses, also titled "Limericks from Yuggoth," appeared in *Crypt of Cthulhu* No 12 (Eastertide 1983) and totals thirteen numbered limericks with a pseudo-scholarly (though humorous) short introduction by Carter. One example will suffice:

> We hardly know aught of Shaggai
> And I find myself wondering why,
>   Since it sounds rather jaunty,
>   And lies so close to Stronti
> That they wave as we Mi-Go flap by.

A second gathering, "More Limericks from Yuggoth" (limericks XIV–XVI), appeared in *Crypt of Cthulhu* No. 18 (Yuletide 1983). The third gathering, "Still More Limericks from Yuggoth," appeared in *Crypt of Cthulhu* No. 51 (Hallowmas 1987). The fourth and final sequence of limericks, "And Yet Even Still More Limericks from Yuggoth" (limericks XXXX–LIV), appeared in *Crypt of Cthulhu* No. 53 (Candlemas 1988).

A second series of connected verses written by Carter in the 1980s (in 1987–88, to be precise) was "The Intelligent Child's Own Book of Interesting and Instructive Monsters"—eight poems about monsters mythological, literary, and invented. The titles were: "The Jabberwock," "The Yeti," "The Leviathan," "The Myrmecoleari," "The Corkodrill," "The Upas," "The Garuda," and "The Ziff." The first two appeared in *Crypt of Cthulhu* No. 52 (Yuletide 1987), the next two No. 53 (Candlemas 1988), poems five and six in No. 55 (Eastertide 1988), and the final two in No. 56 (Roodmas 1988).

Carter resided in East Orange, New Jersey, in his final years. In 1985, he developed oral cancer, leading to his death in 1988, and died in nearby Montclair. The year of Carter's death, Charnel House Chapbooks of Mount Olive, North Carolina (an imprint of Robert M. Price's Cryptic Publications), issued the slim chapbook *Visions from Yaddith* in an edition of 200 numbered copies only, with a facsimile of Carter's signature. This slim pamphlet contains eleven numbered poems in blank verse, as follows: "I. Dreams in the Dark"; "II. The Peril from Below"; "III. The Mage Nzoorka"; "IV. The Fumblers at the Gate"; "V. The Gathering Place"; "V. The Searchers from Afar"; "VII. The Return to Yaddith"; "VIII. The Word from Abbith"; "IX. The City Falls"; "X. To Worlds Afar"; "XI. The Prophecy." The poems tell the story of the race of the Nug-

Soth, mages who inhabit planet Yaddith, and the threat posed to the survival of their race by Dhole-things, great swine-snouted worms that can track the Nug-Soth even through their dreams.

Robert M. Price provides an introduction in which he relays Carter's fabricated history of the volume, first introduced as a central motif in Carter's story "Dreams in the House of Weir," in which fragments of the poems are quoted. This tale first appeared in an anthology edited by Carter, *Weird Tales* No. 1 (Zebra Books, 1980), and was reprinted posthumously in the Robert M. Price anthology *The Shub-Niggurath Cycle* (Chaosium, 1994), along with the complete "Visions from Yaddith" poetry sequence. According to Carter's story, the slim folio of verse was supposedly penned by a female poet, Ariel Prescott. Prescott was clearly either English or resident in England, for Carter's tale tells us that the poetry "had enjoyed a mild vogue among the [Cambridge] undergraduates— those of them given to sampling hashish and studying occultism and Theosophy at any rate . . ." The volume had been issued in 1927 by London's Charnel House Publishers, but her family had bought up and destroyed all the known copies. At least one survived to be discovered by Winfield Phillips in Carter's tale "The Winfield Inheritance." The author eventually died (as is the common fate of such macabre poets) raving in a madhouse. This is clearly all Carter's variant on the theme of the shocking volumes of weird poetry authored by Edwin Pickman Derby in Lovecraft's "The Thing on the Doorstep" and Justin Geoffrey's *People of the Monolith* in Howard's "The Black Stone." And let us remember that Abdul Alhazred was not merely the author of the *Necronomicon*, but "a mad poet."

Carter published several more poems toward the end of his life. *Crypt of Cthulhu* No. 26 (Hallowmas 1984) published "Susran" and No. 36 (Yuletide 1985) "High Atlantis." "Mu" was published in *Weird Tales* 50, No. 4 (Winter 1988/89), as was "Sabbat Eve" in the same issue. *Weird Tales* also published "Walpurgisnacht" in its Fall 1988 issue. Two poems appeared in the fanzine *Spectral Tales* (another production of Robert M. Price's Cryptic Publications): "Fear" in 1, No. 1 (June 1988) and "Druid Hill" in the December 1989 issue. It is clear the thematic focus of his poetry remained myth, legend, and exotica, as in his earliest days of writing verse.

A few other Carter poems have appeared posthumously. "Moorceffoc" appeared in *Fungi* No. 17 (1998) and "The Song of Laine the Dreamer," one of Carter's earliest published poems, was reprinted by editor/publisher James van Hise in his *Sword and Fantasy* No. 2 (April 2005).

The critical reception of Carter's verse has thus far been poor. S. T. Joshi has expressed the view that Carter's poetry is "derivative" of Smith, Lovecraft, Dunsany, and Howard, and that his prose writing is "sadly derivative" of Smith, Howard, James Branch Cabell, and other writers. (*Sixty Years of Arkham House* 136). There is, indeed, no denying these clear literary influences on Carter's verse.

Carter's literary executor, Robert M. Price, has a mixed but overall negative opinion of Carter's efforts in the realm of poetry. Of the poems in *Dreams from R'lyeh,* Price states:

> Carter is a skilful rhymer (though some of the lines scan only if you pronounce certain Mythos names as the original authors probably did not intend), but to me the sonnets seem uninspired, lacking in truly poetic diction. They read like prose that happens to rhyme. And unlike the poetry of Lovecraft, Rimel, Smith and Lowndes which they seek to emulate, the *Dreams from R'lyeh* do not seem to have the magical quality of evocativeness. Carter's verses do not point beyond the page. For the most part they are merely rehashes of stock Mythos features that the knowing reader has heard a hundred times. They share with Carter's fiction the flaw of being grossly over-explicit, throwing slime, putrescence, and tentacles at the reader coming and going. If such a lack of subtlety severely impedes fiction, it is fatal to poetry. (*Lin Carter* 100)

A damning assessment indeed!

L. Sprague de Camp was kinder to his friend's poetry in the introduction to *Dreams from R'lyeh*. Though claiming no great artistic significance to the verse, he writes:

> Nowadays, if he does not amuse or entertain, the poet might as well keep his verses to himself for all the attention that will be paid him. Nobody is going to solve such intractable prob-

lems as war and peace, the production and distribution of wealth, and the relations between the sexes by writing poems about them - least of all poems that sound as if composed by a computer - although some contemporary poems seem to think they ought to try. So let's have some poems that are fun to read. That means poems that say their say in intelligible English and that exploit, rather than are constrained by, the devices of fixed forms to strengthen their impact. As, for instance, the present collection. (xii–xiii)

Price is as dismissive of *Visions from Yaddith* as he is of the work in *Dreams from R'lyeh*. He writes: "Here again, the merely exotic tries to do the work of the evocative and inevitably fails. The jarring sprinkling of pulp science fiction and horror jargon works like evil magic to banish whatever mood might otherwise arise" (100). It must be admitted that sequence is probably amongst Carter's poorest. The complete absence of regular metre makes the use of the blank verse undisciplined and sloppy-seeming.

Of Carter's limericks, Price writes:

I am tempted to suggest that the third set of Mythos poems, the fifty-four Limericks from Yuggoth, is the most effective, since the least pretentious of the three. Some of these are awful, others quite funny, and the whole idea of reducing the sublime sonnet cycle to a ludicrous limerick sequence is itself hilarious . . . Lin was not, and did not necessarily pretend to be, the originator of the Lovecraftian limerick. That honor may belong to "Morbius M. Moamrath" (pen name of Joseph Pumilia and Bill Wallace). Darrell Schweitzer discusses their limerick-cycle *A Young Guy from Fuggoth* in his survey article "Supernatural Humour in Literature," *Crypt of Cthulhu*, No. 61 (1988). (*Lin Carter* 100, 104)

(Schweitzer himself has published several chapbooks of humorous Lovecraftian verse.)

It may be that Price is inclined to appreciate Carter's limericks more than his other verse, since he himself was inspired to write two sequences of Lovecraftian limericks. "Mildew from Shaggai" (a sequence of thirty numbered limericks) and "Shards from Shaggai" (a sequence of twenty-five numbered limericks) appear in Price's anthology *Black Forbidden Things* along with the entirety of Carter's "Limericks from Yuggoth" sequence.

The rear jacket flap of *Dreams from R'lyeh* proclaims that Carter's writings

> have aroused the enthusiasm of Arkham House patrons, who recognise in them a subtle artistry of pure stylistic mastery by a writer who has [more] successfully captured the flavor and mood and color of Lovecraft and Clark Ashton Smith than has any other writer of Carter's generation . . . The central sonnet-cycle, of course, is an affectionate and knowing imitation of Lovecraft's own "Fungi from Yuggoth" sequence, skilfully written . . .

Perhaps this appraisal, no doubt written by August Derleth, was too lavish in its praise. Nevertheless, many enthusiasts of these great fantasy writers enjoy well-handled pastiche of their style and themes, and Carter's poetic oeuvre provides pleasures via evoking echoes of them.

That Carter had a firm grasp of both meter and rhyme (both essentials of traditional formalist verse), and of such devices as alliteration, and of a variety of poetic forms, is amply demonstrated by both his own verse and by his review of Richard L. Tierney's volume *Collected Poems: Nightmares and Visions* (Arkham House, 1981); see *Crypt of* Cthulhu No. 22 (Roodmas 1984): 53, where Carter, despite his praise for Tierney's talents overall, does not hesitate to call out incorrect scansion in certain lines, the occasional false rhyme and so on.

While Carter's verse is certainly uneven in quality, his place as a poet of the fantasy field and his body of work deserve more appreciation. Certainly *Dreams from R'lyeh* (the sequence) holds its place with such more recent *Fungi from Yuggoth*–inspired sequences as Michael Fantina's *Flowers from Nithon* and Leigh Blackmore's *Spores from Sharnoth*. A full critical appraisal of Carter's entire poetic oeuvre still awaits, and may require the assemblage of a volume of his *Complete Fantastic Poems*. Now there is a project for an enterprising publisher!

Robert M. Price notes that one of Carter's many planned projects that unfortunately never came to fruition was

Innsmouth Jewelry, a slim volume collecting Lovecraft's *Fungi from Yuggoth,* Rimel's *Dreams of Yith,* Lowndes's *Annals of Arkhya,* and others. He writes: "The title is perfect, as Lovecraft described the antique jewelry of the Deep Ones as exceedingly fine, exotically beautiful, yet disturbingly outré" (*Lin Carter* 104). This volume could also still be published, and would make a worthwhile addition to the library of any Lovecraftian enthusiast or weird poetry fan.

Works Cited or Consulted

Carter, Lin. *Dreams from R'lyeh.* Sauk City, WI: Arkham House, 1975.

Fancyclopedia 3: fancyclopedia.org/Fancyclopedia_3.

Jaffery, Sheldon. *The Arkham House Companion: Fifty Years of Arkham House &c.* Mercer Island, WA: Starmont House, 1989.

Joshi, S. T. *Sixty Years of Arkham House: A History and Bibliography.* Sauk City, WI: Arkham House, 1999.

Neilson, Leon. *Arkham House: A Collector's Guide.* Jefferson, NC: McFarland, 2004.

Price, Robert M. *Lin Carter: A Look Behind His Imaginary Worlds.* San Bernardino, CA: Borgo Press, 1991.

———, ed. *Black Forbidden Things: Cryptical Secrets from the "Crypt of Cthulhu."* Mercer Island, WA; Starmont House, 1992.

———, ed. *The Xothic Legend Cycle: The Complete Mythos Fiction of Lin Carter.* Oakland, CA: Chaosium, 1997.

Servello, Stephen J., ed. *Apostle of Letters: A Critical Evaluation of the Works of Lin Carter.* [Winchester, VA:] WildCat Books, 2006.

I would like to thank Bobby Derie for providing me with a copy of the Charnel House Chapbook text of Carter's *Visions from Yaddith*.

June Ruins Everything

Short Reviews of Streaming Horror Film and Television for the Covid Era

June Pulliam

During the pandemic, I have been hard at work, watching horror film and television, the good, the bad, and the ugly, so you don't have to. What follows is a series of short reviews of what's out there on Amazon Prime, Hulu, HBO, Showtime, CBS, Netflix, Shudder, and PBS.

The Cured. David Freyne, dir. 2017.

The BBC series *In the Flesh* (2013–14) did it first and better than this Irish film, which is a take on the zombie for the Covid generation. As in Danny Boyle's *28 Days Later* (2002), a virus turns the living into mindless ravening fiends. But thanks to science, 75% of those infected the virus can be cured. However, the cured cannot resume their former lives because the uninfected survivors of the zombie pandemic will never forgive them for what they did while infected. While the formerly infected can remember every terrible thing they did before they were cured, they are also upset about how they are scorned and discriminated against, as well as the target of Karens. This situation makes for lots of bad feelings and revenge on both sides. *In the Flesh* did it better in how it humanized the infected and explored how they process their own guilt over what they did before they were cured and how their families and their victims process their anger and grief.

What We Do in the Shadows. (2019–) FX.

Vampires are dicks: they are completely selfish, and their familiars are codependents, which is surprisingly hilarious. This FX series is based on the 2014 mockumentary of the same name, but I think the series is much more enjoyable than the original. For one thing, it stars the hilarious British actor Matt Barry, who is also the star of *The Toast of London* (2012–

20). *What We Do in the Shadows* also includes a variety of vampires and wannabes ranging from ancient Eastern European immortal warlords to an emotional vampire who can drain people with his preternatural ability of boring people to death.

The Walking Dead. (2010–23) AMC.

I thought that *The Walking Dead* was done when I watched the last few episodes in March in the early days of lockdown. The whole of season 10 was perfunctory: they writers and showrunners seemed to be sick of this show that should have ended in Season 8. That was sad, since the Whisperers had the potential to be interesting characters in their own right. While Rick's group (less Rick, and Maggie for the past few seasons) was clearly trying to set up a new civilization based on American values where the living and the walkers are natural enemies, Beta and the Whisperers had post-human qualities that would have been interesting if the show had invested enough time in exploring them. Once you get past the ick-factor of how the Whisperers pass among the dead by wearing their faces, their philosophy of living among the walkers as a new form of life is intriguing. So imagine my surprise when in September I learned that there were two more episodes of *The Walking Dead* left in what I thought was to be the penultimate season. Beta was defeated, and the two groups went their separate ways. Admittedly, this was not much of a denouement, but it was something. Then I learned in a *USA Today* article (9 September 2020) that AMC has given the series one more season that will consist of twenty-four episodes concluding in 2023. Why? There is nothing left in the original *Walking Dead* universe, whose storyline shuffles along like a zombie. Additionally, AMC announced that two more spinoff series will join the franchise's original spinoff, *Fear the Walking Dead*. A yet-unnamed spinoff will center around Daryl (Norman Reedus) and Carol (Melissa McBride), and a scripted anthology series *Tales of the Walking Dead* will feature individual episodes with stories about existing characters, backstories, or other stand-alone stories. Additionally, a trilogy of films built around the show's original leading character, Rick (Andrew Lincoln), are in the works via

Universal Pictures. I hope that the two new series and planned film trilogy are not just another version of *Fear the Walking Dead,* whose only contribution to the franchise that I can see was to start the series in the first days of the zombie apocalypse. Otherwise, *TWD* has become the zombie that just won't die.

Chopping Mall. Jim Wynorski, dir. 1986.

If *Dawn of the Dead* and *Robocop* had a baby, it would be Chopping Mall. As the title suggests, the ensuing horrors are set in a mall, but without *Dawn's* critique of the pre-Internet cathedral of consumer capitalism or *Robocop's* depiction of worker consciousness hijacked by capitalism. *Chopping Mall's* slasher is not a deranged human, but a squad of security robots who terminate with extreme prejudice several teens who hide in the mall until closing so that they can use the facilities as their own private playground. *Chopping Mall* is one of a stream of formulaic slasher films that were produced in the 1980s—post–*Texas Chainsaw Massacre* Final Girl character and pre-metatextual *Scream.* The film's title tells you everything that you need to know about what will happen.

The Comedy of Terrors. Jacques Tourneur, dir. 1963.

This campy 1960s version of Grand Guignol came to my attention on Amazon Prime, and when I saw that Vincent Price starred, I decided that *The Comedy of Terrors* might be a good way to pass an otherwise dull evening.

Vincent Price was a national treasure. Fight me.

But even with Price in the leading role, however, I was prepared to be underwhelmed by this film, which I thought would be too durative of 1960s comic horror classics such as *The Ghost and Mr. Chicken* starring another national treasure, Don Knotts.

I was wrong. Horror veteran Jacques Tourneur directs 1930s and 1940s horror and suspense luminaries Peter Lorre, Boris Karloff, and Basil Rathbone in this film, with a script written by Richard Matheson. Lorre, Karloff, Rathbone, and Price give delightful performances as parodic versions of the characters who made each famous. *The Comedy of Terrors* also stars Orangey the cat, the only feline winner of the Patsy

Award, which is the animal equivalent of an Oscar. Some of you might recognize Orangey from his previous work, such as the unneutered ginger tom who chased Scott Carey into the basement in Jack Arnold's *The Incredible Shrinking Man* (1957), based on Richard Matheson's novella *The Shrinking Man,* or in *Breakfast at Tiffany's* (1961) as Audrey Hepburn's co-star. Audrey played shitty pet parent Holly Golightly's, who couldn't even bother to give her cat a better name than "Cat."

The Comedy of Terrors revives horror tropes from an earlier time, such as Resurrection Men, who made their living by supplying cadavers to medical schools. Price plays Waldo Trumbull, an unscrupulous undertaker whose job allows him to engage in the resurrection business without having to dig up the corpses. Part of the film's comedy lies in the Trumbulls' loveless marriage, which is marred by constant the couple's constant bickering.

All these elements make *The Comedy of Terrors* a film that deserves more attention.

The Masque of the Red Death. Roger Corman, dir. 1964.

Vincent Prince also stars in this Hammer Studio's take on Edgar Allan Poe's short story of the same name. Price plays a cruel aristocrat who parties as if it's 1999. After he demands that his serfs give him all the food that they have stored to survive the winter, Prince Prospero burns their homes to stop the spread of the coming plague, which he plans on weathering in his castle with some of his aristocrat friends. Of course, the red death finds its way into Prospero's fortress, killing everyone. Price's copious stage, screen, radio, and even television experience allowed him to give artful performances of vicious, cruel men who were both over-the-top and believable.

An added bonus to *The Masque of the Red Death* is Hammer Studio's signature use of color in their films produced between the 1950s and early '70s. Amy Anna comments on them in the online journal *Cut. Print. Film.*, where she explains how Hammer at this time used "eye-popping, lush, sensual color" both as a way to tell stories and also just for pure gorgeous eye candy and visual effect ("A Study of Scarlet: Color in Hammer Horror Films," 2015). Hammer's use of primary and secondary color in films from its classic era is hypnotic, beyond any technicolor extravaganza of the time.

Dr. Jekyll and Sister Hyde. Ray Ward Baker, dir. 1971.

Hammer Studio's version of Robert Louis Stevenson's novel is a gender-bending mashup of fictional characters and real Victorians who could be found London's East End, even if the story's history is a bit off. Dr. Henry Jekyll sets out to create the elixir of life from female hormones, and the elixir looks suspiciously like absinthe, particularly since Jekyll experiments on himself with his elixir by tossing it back in a crystal goblet. Jekyll's elixir does not so much prolong youth as it sets free his inner female psychopath. When Jekyll drinks his elixir, he changes into a beautiful woman whose libido is superior to his own. He passes off this second self as Mrs. Hyde, his widowed sister who has come to stay with him. When Jekyll needs more female cadavers to continue compounding his elixir, he must procure them himself, as the infamous resurrectionists Burke and Hare are no longer in the business after Burke has been lynched by an angry mob for murdering women and selling their bodies to medical schools. (Never mind that Burke and Hare did their grisly work, in Edinburgh, sixty years before the real time of the film.) Since Jack the Ripper has just begun his Whitechapel murder spree, Jekyll's kills are attributed to the infamous and still unknown murderer. After a man fitting Jekyll's description is spotted in the area after one of the murders, Mrs. Hyde takes his place, finding and killing women to serve as cadavers in Jekyll's lab.

This Hammer production also exemplifies the studio's unique use of color, particularly the shade of primary red used to represent blood. While human blood is a warmer and sometimes deeper shade of red, Hammer's bluish-red blood splashed across its victims stands out amidst the greens, yellows, pinks, and cobalt blues that were part of the studio's regular palette. Mrs. Hyde's red dress matches this shade of blood exactly.

But the film's most distinctive aspect is the monster's queerness. Through Mrs. Hyde, Henry can express his desire for his best friend Howard in a way that Henry never could in his own body. True, this desire is expressed in the body of a woman who ticks all the boxes of monstrous femininity, but Mrs. Hyde is also very much part of Dr. Jekyll, who loses consciousness when he uses his elixir to transition into a female body. Mrs. Hyde retains her male double's intelligence as well as his scruples about murdering prostitutes in order to advance the scientific greater good. In one scene, after Jekyll has resumed his male form while Mrs. Hyde controls his consciousness, Jekyll meets Howard on the street and caresses his face, which very much confuses the cis het Howard. I can't think of an American horror film made during this time that so openly represented bisexual and homosexual desire.

The Strangers: Prey at Night. Johannes Roberts, dir. 2018.

If you've never seen a slasher film, you might like this film. Otherwise. *The Strangers* is one big yawnfest. There is absolutely nothing original about the plot. The killers kill because, in the words of one, "why not?" There's a final girl, but the plot is so derivative that I didn't care if she survived. Christina Hendricks is in *The Strangers*. Fortunately for her, she is killed midway through, or her character is. The only good thing I can say about *The Strangers* is that it gave employment to people in the film industry.

Little Joe. Jessica Hausner, dir. 2019.

In this updated version of *Invasion of the Body Snatchers*, a genetically engineered flower (Little Joe) releases pollen that co-opts the human brain. The pollen prompts the human brain to release endorphins so that humans will do anything to protect the plant. Even better, those exposed to Little Joe's pollen become calmer, more interested in romantic love than their careers, as well as less overprotective of their children. Those who realize how Little Joe changes people and try to destroy the flowers are the villains in this film, such as Bella, a sad older woman who attempted suicide a year before and has since gotten an emotional support dog. When Bella's dog breathes Little Joe's pollen, she swears that he's changed—her formerly overcontrolled canine companion now growls at Bella and bites her. This prompts Bella to take her once-beloved dog to the vet to get that final shot. Believing that her dog is no longer "her dog" or the "same dog," Bella takes her beloved pet to the vet to be euthanized. Seriously? If I got upset every time a dog of mine nipped me then I would never have a Chihuahua.

However, Little Joe's creator, Alice, is more sympathetic than her colleague Bella. Little Joe is named after her son, and at first she believes that the plant is so benign that she brings home one to give to her son. When Alice realizes what Little Joe is doing to the human brain, she tries to persuade her male colleagues of the dangers of the GMO plant that will make them and the company the work for wealthy. Unfortunately for Alice, her male colleagues are a bunch of patronizing pricks who try to gaslight her, and I am not gonna blame their behavior on huffing Little Joe's pollen. I've dealt with men like this before. They are the reason that women are underrepresented in science. In one of *Little Joe*'s final scenes, Alice is dragged into the greenhouse by one of her male colleagues, who pulls down her mask to forcibly infect her. This bro perfectly predicts today's anti-maskers who are the reason we can't have nice things, like health. But Alice does not get infected with Covid and die on a ventilator. Instead, after her colleague has roofied her with Little Joe dust, she "loosens up" and indicates her willingness to become romantically involved with this man whose advances she had previously scorned. What makes Little Joe's ending so horrific is how the patriarchy or its idea of a biological imperative prevails by means of a boy plant that mellows out everyone, making a visit by the "suede denim secret police" unnecessary.

Kudos to director and co-writer Jessica Hausner's filmmaking. *Little Joe* is a subtle horror film that defies easy classification. I'm not even sure the term horror really applies. *Little Joe* only made approximately $200,000 worldwide, and I assume that it was made on a low budget due to the lack of special effects and big-name stars. But these are not failings. The small amount of physical violence in the film always occurs off-screen, which makes it much more disturbing. And Hausner uses stark sets lit with bright colors to imply futurity, danger, and desire. Hausner proves that you don't need these things to make an original and engrossing film.

Black Christmas. Bob Clark, dir. 1974.

This Canadian horror film is still an original addition to the slasher film genre. The film's ending lacks so much closure that its original material was never milked for endless sequels along the model of the *Halloween, Nightmare on Elm Street,* and *Friday the 13th* franchises.

But the most horrifying element of *Black Christmas* is that the film could be taking place today. Even before the murderer, who is never identified and caught, begins terrorizing the women of Phi Kappa Epsilon, their lives are permeated by male violence and control. Women are killed for failing to fit into narrow norms of femininity: they walk by themselves, they have sex with their boyfriends, they drink, they swear, they are bawdy, or they are even old—all typical slasher film fare. But other slasher films from this era do not depict how women are coerced into oppressive feminine norms and punished even if they do conform. On the night that the first sister and house mother of Phi Kappa Epsilon are murdered and their bodies dragged into the attic where the unidentified slasher uses their bodies to play out his ill-defined childhood, he also murders a twelve-year-old girl in the park. What "crime" could a twelve-year-old girl be guilty of, in slasher film logic, to merit her murder? The women of Phi Kappa Epsilon regularly receive what are euphemistically described as "obscene" phone calls, which resemble invective-laced tirades against all womenkind of the sort exemplified by Rep. Ted Yoho against Alexandria Ocasio-Cortez or rabid anti-feminist attorney Den Hollander, who recently murdered the son of federal judge Esther Salas during his failed attempt to gain entry into her home to kill her.

When several of the women of Phi Kappa Epsilon prevail on the police to locate the missing twelve-year-old girl along with their missing sister Clare, who never made it to meet her father, or to do something about the threatening phone calls, the all-male law enforcement officers dismiss their concerns. Clare is just "shacking up" somewhere with a boyfriend, the twelve-year-old hasn't been missing long enough, and the caller is probably just one of the "girl's" boyfriends playing a joke. The police refuse to investigate until Clare's father and her boyfriend come to the police station and insist that they do so. Even Clare's father is oppressive and judgmental. He is horrified to learn that just the night before, the women of Phi Kappa Epsilon were drinking alcohol their tame Christmas party, and that his daughter had a boyfriend.

Jess, the film's final girl, is not a virgin in the tradition of women who survive the maniac's wrath in this genre of film. She's pregnant and planning on having an abortion over the objections of her boyfriend Peter, who calls her a "selfish bitch" for wanting to continue her education instead of her pregnancy. And Jess does not put up with anyone's bullshit: she insists that the police investigate the harassing phone calls coming into the sorority house, and she tells her boyfriend Peter that he has no right to tell her what to do with her body. Jess is not like her fragile friend Phyl, who cries about everything, but she is also stronger than the profane Barb, who is drunk for most of the film and enjoys making men uncomfortable with her sexual innuendo. Later, when Peter breaks into the house to have another "talk" with Jess about her pregnancy, she mistakes him for the slasher and quite capably dispatches him. Jess's ability to survive the entire film is due to her skill at navigating a world that is hostile to women. Nearly fifty years later in the #MeToo era, Jess is relatable because women are still dealing with the same macro- and micro-aggressions from men and fighting to control their bodies.

June Pulliam is a goddamned delight. But she ruins everything because she doesn't give spoiler alerts.

Devil's Night Investigated: An Interview with Curtis M. Lawson

Géza A. G. Reilly

CURTIS M. LAWSON. *Devil's Night*. Weird House Press, 2020. 214 pp. $45.00 hc. ISBN: 978-1-888993-06-6.

I was thrilled to have the opportunity to interview Curtis M. Lawson about his recent *Devil's Night,* which is a collection of twelve stories and two vignettes all set in Detroit, Michigan, on 30 October 1987. The collection is named for a formerly annual event in Detroit that saw petty and serious crime, including arson, run rampant. The city was able to bring the yearly sprees to an end in the mid-1990s, but the idea of Devil's Night had already made its way into the popular consciousness, helped in no small part by J. O'Barr's *The Crow* and its film adaptation. In Lawson's collection, of course, readers are treated to Devil's Night as focused through the lens of weird flair.

The following interview was conducted over Facebook Messenger over a period of several weeks. As little of the text has been altered as possible; my contributions have been edited to excise extraneous commentary, leaving only the questions intact wherever possible, and Lawson's answers have only been edited to correct the occasional typographical error. My thanks again to Curtis M. Lawson for his time and forbearance.

* * *

GR: Your stories are linked in several ways (aside from just the setting), some subtly, some overtly. However, there was one connection I couldn't figure out: why 1987 specifically?

CML: I chose 1987 because it was right around the height of Devil's Night. There were an extraordinary number of fires that year. By the early '90s, things had started to slow down, and there was less and less arson. I tried to foreshadow that a little bit in the final story in the collection without explicitly stating what the future held.

Also, Devil's night was on a weekend that year, so it kind of worked out for stuff like the younger characters staying up late and such. I know most people wouldn't have checked what day of the week 30 October 1987 was, but someone would have.

GR: I'm curious about your use of the urban legends of Detroit (the Nain Rouge, the Pig Lady, etc.). To what extent were you able to put your own stamp on these legends? Was it difficult to keep them from pushing your own interpretations of them out, or was it easy to give them your authorial "voice"?

CML: One of the cool things about working with urban legends and with myth is that there are enough different versions and contradictory accounts that you can kind of cherrypick the parts that work for your story and even use the contradictions to create a kind of mysterious, disorienting atmosphere. That's what I tried to do with the Nain Rouge. In one story, he provides the means for karmic justice. In most he is a bad omen or even malevolent. All that fits one account or another.

As for the Hobo Pig Lady, I couldn't find any written accounts, just word-of-mouth stories from Detroit locals. I had to take greater liberties with her because of that, but the lack of written lore about her gave me a lot of freedom to make her my own.

GR: You certainly don't shy away from displaying the social inequality that plagued (and still plagues) Detroit, particularly in terms of the poverty that affected the city after the White Flight of the 1960s and the auto industry largely pulled out of the state. Based on what I've read of your work, you don't seem like the sort of author who'd shy away from incorporating analogies for real-world conditions into your horrors. Was it important to you to have your stories work on the level of analogy and address the inequality that's run throughout Detroit's modern history?

CML: It wasn't so much that I wanted to make a statement as much as I wanted to be genuine. I did a lot of research into Detroit and its history. Inequality is a big part of that history. It would be silly and disingenuous to pretend otherwise.

There's a saying about how fiction is a lie that tells the truth, and I think that's true even in fantastical stories. I wanted to examine real issues and the harsh reality of the setting in an honest way, even if the stories are about magic dice and half-demons fighting priests.

I wouldn't say that I was motivated by any sort of attempt at literary activism or any such thing. I'm a firm believer that great fiction addresses problems without giving answers. I see it as my job to challenge people *to* think (in an entertaining way), not to tell them *what* to think.

GR: In terms of your research, what did you rely on? Traditional histories? Social histories of individual communities within Detroit as a whole? More stuff from the fringe that focused on Detroit's urban legend underbelly?

CML: I read a nonfiction book called *Devil's Night and Other True Tales of Detroit*. [It] had a lot of interesting anecdotes that I drew from, including stories about Chaldean merchants facing violent racism from black communities where they owned small stores. It also got into the kind of seedy underbelly of the Motown music scene and showed how the city could devour anyone, regardless of their standing.

I did a lot of online research for legends and myths, but I also reached out to locals and asked about any stories I might have never heard of and for details about the atmosphere, geography, etc.

Old news footage and YouTube videos were a good source of inspiration and info. I watched interviews with cops and dealers. I watched footage of old fires and lists of supposedly haunted spots in Michigan. Anything I could find.

I also studied a lot of maps and satellite images. Detroit is interesting from a planning and layout perspective. I grew up around Boston, and everything is a mess here. We just built it as we went. Detroit is deliberate.

GR: Have you managed to visit Detroit, or other areas in Michigan, in the past? Related to that, was any part of your collection a riff off of firsthand experience by the author (even if that experience didn't actually occur in Detroit)?

CML: I've driven through Michigan and I've had a layover at the airport there, but that's it.

As for firsthand experiences, there were a few I drew from. Growing up, my parents were big party types. They were always drinking and doing drugs and often had kind of scummy friends over. I'd hide in my room and play music and lose myself in comics, D&D manuals, etc. [The story] "D20" reflected a lot of my childhood coping mechanisms.

[The story] "A Night of Art and Excess" draws on some of my emotional history. Up until my late twenties, I always lived in kind of bad urban neighborhoods (so I guess there is another thing I drew from), and when I was younger, I felt like I shouldn't have been there, like it was some cosmic mistake. I had this idea in my head that I was cut from a different kind of cloth, that I was one of the elites, and the world just didn't know it yet. It's kind of a childish coping psychological response to the depressing realities of growing up poor. I see that in hindsight, but it's a feeling I'm intimately familiar with. You can see that same theme in a different way in *Black Heart Boys' Choir*.

And then there was my time in California as a kid. I was there for the Rodney King riots. I lived in Long Beach, and you could see the smoke over Los Angeles from my window. And then there was all the violence on the news. That experience definitely influenced some of the emotional atmosphere in *Devil's Night*.

GR: For some reason, I'd gotten it into my head that you'd been a lifelong resident of New England. You mention in the introduction to *Devil's Night* that there are several literary and cultural influences that crop up in the stories. Though you never went for outright pastiche, the influence of Lovecraft on "Devil's Tongue" and J. O'Barr on "Through Hell for One Kiss" felt fairly obvious. What other writers or artists made their impression upon your stories here, do you think, and how did they complement your vision of Detroit?

CML: I've lived in New England most of my life. I spent a year in California. My dad was sent there for a special project (he was a naval engineer).

As for influences, "The Graveyard of Charles Robert Swede" was loosely modeled on "The Willows" by Algernon Blackwood (the last name "Swede" being a nod to one of the characters in that story). "The Willows" is one of the best examples of using the setting in an antagonistic fashion, so I tried to capture that kind of feeling for Detroit.

Frank Miller's *Sin City* was a big influence. I had always wanted to do something like that where the stories all kind of connect in small ways and where the setting becomes almost a character itself. I actually mentioned *Sin City* in the pitch for *Devil's Night*.

You were right on Lovecraft and O'Barr, of course. Lovecraft influences almost everything I do, and *The Crow* sparked my interest in Devil's Night and first introduced me to the concept of "urban Gothic" (for lack of a better term).

I suppose the idea of Gothic literature in general informed the book, too. One of the key elements of Gothic fiction is the idea of a house in decay—something once great that has fallen. That sounds like Detroit.

I drew from some music too. There is a band called Botanist. They have all this "floral Apocalypse" imagery, and that put the ideas for the plant monsters and the vines throughout the stories on my head. I just fell in love with the imagery in their music and wanted to capture that in prose.

GR: I found it a bit difficult to get a sense of Detroit as a city from your stories, since each of them were focused on individual, almost intimate, corners of the landscape. This is not to say that Detroit wasn't recognizable or anything; it's just that the city felt, to me, like it was being seen in snapshots rather than in one comprehensible total image, as though the scale was missing in some way. Was that intentional on your part?

CML: Kind of. In one of the books I read about Detroit it talks about how back before white flight, the city was broken into almost tribal-like areas. There was a black section, a Jewish section, a Polish section, etc. Each was almost like its own little town.

Even today, the city is broken up into these kinds of distinct districts. So I was trying to illustrate that to a certain degree. And then in "A Night of Art and Excess," I wanted to give more of an aerial view, so to speak, showing the view of the city below from the heights of the privileged few.

GR: Was your use of vignettes, like "Fire Sermon" and "Rashaam the Unholy," intended to further that sense of demarcation, that sense of a "snapshot" Detroit, or was there another reason for including them alongside the longer narratives?

CML: I did want to do little snapshot pieces, but also, I just kind of like writing small pieces like that. I find them to be a nice break sometimes, as a reader and as a writer.

I had some similar pieces in my first collection, and a few people seemed to really like them. Hopefully, it doesn't disrupt the flow for anyone.

GR: How did you envision this collection? Had you sketched out ideas for any of the stories before realizing that you wanted to write an entire collection on Devil's Night in Detroit? Or did the concept come before the stories?

CML: The concept came first. S. T. Joshi had put me in contact with Joe Morey at Weird House Press. He had recommended *Black Heart Boys' Choir* to Joe for publication. Joe passed as he didn't feel the book was right for his press, but he asked me to pitch him a collection. He suggested a Halloween collection as an idea. I thought Devil's Night would be more interesting, so I ran it by him, and we went with it.

GR: Was the process of creating a collection of interrelated narratives (sometimes overtly interrelated, sometimes tacitly) different, or more difficult, than your process of creating a novel usually is? If so, how?

CML: I followed a similar process. I'm more comfortable with long-form fiction than short stuff. I like outlining novels and figuring out the puzzle of how to connect this scene to that, how to intertwine recurring themes and symbolism, etc. One of the reasons I chose to connect these stories was because it gave me a structure to work within and an artistically valid reason to include motifs and recurring symbols from one story to another.

My process is very deliberate and planned out. I use color-coded note cards to track plot threads, character arcs, etc. It was a bit less structured for *Devil's Night,* but not by that much.

It's similar to why I prefer writing structured poetry. If I don't have some kind of scaffolding to build upon, I kind of meander and wind up with non-stories.

GR: Did your reliance on strong overall structure make it more difficult to integrate stories that had different internal structures? For example, I'm thinking of how "Trash-Fire Stories" is essentially a *conte cruel,* while "This City Needs Jesus" is a pulp horror/action story, and (as you noted) "The Graveyard of Charles Robert Swede" is weird fiction through and through.

CML: No, that was one of the reasons the structure and overall theme appealed to me, actually. It gave me free rein to tell several different kinds of dark fiction stories but still have them fit together nicely. I went into it wanting to explore several different kinds of horror narratives, and the structure allowed that.

GR: It seems to me that the majority of the overarching story of the collection can be explained by the action of "Devil's Tongue" and "The Exorcism of Detroit, Michigan." However, not every story here fits into the structure of your fictional Detroit painted by those two stories (I'm thinking of

"Rashaam the Unholy," "This City Needs Jesus," and "An Angel in Amber Leaves" specifically). Does the presence of those stories suggest the possibility of future linked works by you set in your Detroit on Devil's Night?

CML: You're definitely right about "Devil's Tongue" and "The Exorcism of Detroit, Michigan." As for the other stories you mentioned, you are onto something as well.

"An Angel in Amber Leaves," in my original manuscript, was the last story, meant to set the stage for Detroit after the Shade creature is destroyed in "Exorcism." I wanted to show that things had changed, but there were still monsters lurking. That's why it takes place on Halloween morning instead of Devil's Night. "This City Needs Jesus" was written with the intention of creating a character I could do more with down the road.

"A Night of Art and Excess" features a character named Edwin Earl Echo who appears in *Black Pantheons* (my first collection), and he is referenced in a few of my other works. Edwin isn't a Detroit-based character though. He goes wherever his muse takes him.

There is definitely the possibility that I may return to Detroit, especially with the character of Adze.

As an aside, there are a few Devil's Night "B-sides" on my Patreon. They are stories that didn't make the final cut for different reasons.

GR: Could you give an example of some of those "B-sides" and discuss why they didn't make the cut for this collection? Is there any chance of including them in an expanded collection, or a Return to Detroit collection, further down the line?

CML: There were four stories that didn't make the final cut. Two of them are unfinished, [and] two of them are finished and up on Patreon.

The unfinished ones just wouldn't cooperate. One of them was about a man who wasn't allowed to die, but it was just too big of a story, and I may turn it into a novella someday. The other one just wouldn't come together.

As for the finished pieces that didn't make it, the short version of the story is that Joe and I didn't think they were as strong as the rest of the collection.

One is called "Gallows of Hell," and it's an adaptation of a comic I wrote about ten years ago. I modified it to fit the Devil's Night theme, but the tone wasn't quite right. It's also fairly derivative—kind of like, what if *The Punisher* went to Hell?

The other story was loosely tied to "D20" and follows the biker who was waiting outside the house and took off when Wolf was killed.

This other biker takes off all scared and crashes. He gets taken, rescued by some folks in a trailer park, and they sacrifice him in a wicker man kind of scenario—something they do each year to protect the park on Devil's Night.

It's a cool story, I think, but it wasn't executed as well as some of the others. I cannibalized the first scene and incorporated some of it into "Breaking Wheel."

GR: "Breaking Wheel" stood out to me. It's almost dead set in the center of the collection (six stories precede it, and seven come after it), and it's one of only two that can be read as entirely non-supernatural. What was the impetus behind that one? Was it a case of the striking visual of Dash up in the air, broken on the wheel as the dawn comes on, coming to you first and then the plot following? Or was there something else behind its creation and inclusion?

CML: I had wanted to do a few non-supernatural stories from the beginning. It goes back to what I said before about this collection giving me the opportunity to explore different facets of horror.

The idea for "Breaking Wheel" came from the idea that poverty and circumstance can grind a person down and bind them. Now, I don't believe that it's like that for everyone, of course. Some folks can claw their way out through determination, smarts, and a bit of luck. Dash isn't one of those people, though.

So I wanted to explore that concept and a breaking wheel

felt like a great metaphor. It was serendipitous that Detroit is laid out in this weird wagon-wheel grid.

I also wanted to explore how poverty and crime manifest in different communities within the same city. I did that a little with "Devil's Tongue," and I came at it from a different angle with "Breaking Wheel."

The characters in both stories have valid reasons to be angry at the world, even if they might not be wholly compatible. In both cases, that anger is toxic and helps trap them in a circle of bad decisions.

GR: It seems that many, if not most, of your characters are affected by or trapped within their own toxicity, walking that line between validity and self-inflicted harm (barring a few notable exceptions, of course). To what extent is your vision of a supernatural Detroit a malign influence, and how much of the conflict in the collection stems from the inherent toxicity of the characters? To put it another way, how much does life suck because, hey, Detroit, and how much does life in Detroit suck because of the people in Detroit?

CML: I suppose, in the case of my fictional Detroit, it's circular. The supernatural toxicity leeches into the people, the people's toxicity impacts those around them, and their toxicity fuels the negative energy that empowers the supernatural undercurrent of the city. So it's like a chicken and egg kind of scenario.

There is a Marvel [comics] character called Blackheart, and he's kind of corny sometimes, but one version of his backstory is that he is a demon spawned by all the negative energy from the crimes committed in this one location. That concept has always stuck with me, and [it] kind of inspired the idea of the "shades" mentioned in "The Exorcism of Detroit, Michigan."

If I had to definitively answer, I would say that there was something dark there to begin with, but it grew stronger with each person's suffering and every cruel act.

On a metaphorical level, it goes back to the cyclical thing. I grew up in a pretty toxic environment, and I let that impact me in a negative way for a long time. It was this wheel of misfortune, and a lot of it was my own doing because I had never been taught how to break out of these patterns. Luckily, I was able to discover my own way out, but a lot of people can't. There's a gravity to these kinds of messed-up lifestyles, especially when you don't know anything else. It's like you know you're in Hell, but you don't know anything else exists. I wanted to express that concept in an interesting, fictional way.

GR: Well, I think I'm about out of questions for you, and I thank you very much for your time and for the fascinating discussion. Is there anything you'd like to say (or, I suppose, ask) to wrap up before we call it a proverbial day?

CML: Nothing I can think of really. I feel you were very thorough.

* * *

Cards-on-the-table time: I was not all that happy with *Devil's Night*. However, I *do* think that I can recommend the book to readers who want a collection themed around such an interesting idea. The one caveat is that should you buy *Devil's Night,* you should be prepared for a work that is adequate, but not exquisite. I was, of course, hoping for the latter based on my reading of Lawson's *Black Heart Boys' Choir,* which *is* exquisite, and was disappointed to not find a work of that caliber here. This is, however, entirely unfair of me, and I realize that my subjective reading of the collection says nothing about its actual merits. Still and all, I am who I am, and thus I think it worthwhile to follow my interview with Lawson with my condensed thoughts on the matter.

The fact is that *Devil's Night* never gelled for me. The stories that make up the collection are interrelated both tacitly (they take place on the same night, after all) and overtly (two stories, at least, are directly linked and define much of the action of the other stories). This is a fine idea, but the fact is that this structure shoots some of its individual components in the foot. For example, an early story, "Devil's Tongue," is written in a wholly unsatisfactory manner where nothing is explained and events, frankly, simply *happen*. It isn't until "The Exorcism of Detroit, Michigan," appearing much later in the collection, that the events of "Devil's Tongue" come into focus. While that sort of setup and payoff would work well in a novel, where ideas and atmosphere can be built up like a sustained note, the structure backfires here. *Devil's Night* is a collection of *stories,* after all, and thus the narratives therein have to be satisfying on an individual level. Sadly, that is too often just not the case for me.

The fact that the whole of *Devil's Night* never comes together for me is compounded by the fact that I felt the most important character—the city of Detroit—never appears on the proverbial stage in a satisfying way. Lawson is adept at drawing his characters, particularly his child characters (who appear with astonishing frequency in *Devil's Night*), but Detroit, which should by all rights be a looming presence in each and every story, never feels as though it were actually *there*. Individual Detroit landmarks do appear, and they're well represented, but the city itself almost fades into the background. Anyone who has been there can tell you that fading away is the one thing Detroit doesn't do. I had expected to come out of *Devil's Night* with some grit of the city under my fingernails, and unfortunately that wasn't the case.

As I've said, my reading of *Devil's Night* is hopelessly tainted by my expectations of Lawson. Those expectations are high because I have been fortunate enough to see what he's capable of, and as a result I couldn't help but be disappointed with his most recent collection. Still and all, my expectations speak only to what's in my head and heart rather than to what's on the page. And what's on the page, all else being equal, is something that I can recommend when the caveats are discarded. If the idea of a themed weird collection intrigues you, if the thought of Devil's Night through a spooky lens grips you, or if you're interested in reading more of Curtis M. Lawson's work, then *Devil's Night* could be for you. An adequate work might not be as satisfying as an exquisite work, but it should be lauded for what it has achieved rather than damned for what it has missed.

The Light That Never Warms
Michael D. Miller

The Lighthouse. Lionsgate, 2019. Directed by Robert Eggers. Starring Robert Pattinson, Willem Dafoe, and Valerlia Karaman.

When Robert Eggers's (*The Witch,* 2015) atmospheric independent film *The Lighthouse* emerged onto the film scene of 2019, it was hailed one of the year's greats (and there were many). This was a film that viewers impressed upon friends because it was "Lovecraftian" (to some) and just hypnotically weird. The film was "art house" cinema, of the kind where viewers had to explain what they watched, what it meant, and why they were weirded out. While the film's merits and its puzzling ending have been enshrined in reviews over the past year, one aspect of this film is its fluid execution of the hallmarks of the weird tale.

The elements most essential to weirdness are mood and atmosphere, layered on line-by-line, paragraph by paragraph, in a sanity-unraveling narrative tale. *The Lighthouse* replicates those elements though a mesmerizing use of sound and image, like the best of the great silent movies (the era, be it noted, in which the weird tale rose to prominence), and like the classics of weird literature, it adds of touch of the cosmic to create horror and wonder.

Like the best of the weird tradition, the premise of the story rests on historical background, which is authenticated to a T with minute detail in the film, from the tools and trappings of the lightkeepers, to their clothing, rations, and mundane daily tasks. According to The Lighthouse Preservation Society:

> Extensive lighthouse construction did not occur in modern times until the 17th century. Prior to that time, most lighthouses were harbor lights serving as homing beacons so boats could safely find their way into port. Beginning in the 17th century, however, as travel on the high seas increased, major

coastal lighthouses were constructed to warn mariners of dangerous rocks, reefs, and currents. Twelve lighthouses were constructed in Britain's American colonies in the 18th century. The first was built in 1716 in Boston Harbor. By 1900 nearly 1,000 lighthouses, both coastal and harbor types, had been built in the United States. Although estimates vary, as many as 50,000 lighthouses may exist in the world today. At the end of the 20th century most of these lighthouses were either automated or abandoned. Before the use of electric beacons, the lighthouse keeper had to keep the gas beacon lit, clean the reflecting mirrors, and remove soot from the tower windows.

Here we have the setting and all the realism needed to set up the weirdness to follow. (It is worth noting Newburyport—inspiration for Lovecraft's Innsmouth—had a lighthouse dating back to 1914 or earlier, though Lovecraft does not mention this.) What is central to the film experience of *The Lighthouse* is contained in the brief historical summary: lighthouses were first home beacons of safety, then became warnings of impending calamity. That is at the heart of the allure of the film: it is simultaneously repulsive and attractive, horror and wonder.

Exploring the weirdness in its sound, *The Lighthouse* opens with a black frame, and a faint but slowly rising woodwind floating in the dark imitates at once the hum of white noise, the song of whales, and perhaps a siren's call. The screen starts to lighten, fading up to a black-and-white shot of an island, floating alone in starless space, and the slender spire of a lighthouse shining out in the void. Then, building upon mood and atmosphere, low deep strings rock in and out like waves or a horn though the fog. The image of this lighthouse attracts because light is a visual sense of hope despite its absence of warmth. Yet we must remember lights can be dangerous: the angler fish luring prey into its maw with an orb-ended appendage that generates a glow, and the very stars that have extinguished themselves long ago, but deceive us. This is image and sound initiating us into weirdness.

We also have an isolated setting that quickly becomes a model of the haunted place. Our two protagonists, Tom Wake

(Dafoe) and Ephraim Winslow (Pattinson), are dropped off on a bare decrepit rock, unstable and alone against the sea, just as we are in the universe. The stark contrast of this is brought out by the orchestrated chiaroscuro of the black-and-white cinematography, at once suggesting age, classicism, and fine art, but also putting us off-kilter for the isolation and conflict of sanity to follow. Our two protagonists also stand in contrast, young and old, the wise and the unwise. As an added touch, Wake inserts his pipe upside down as he exits the screen. (Casting Pattinson in the role of Winslow also adds a strange, unpredictable merit.)

Inside, the festival of image and sound continues. In scenes of still silence we hear turning gears of the light orb, sealing us in. The keeper's room has cramped angles, split in half, two dimensions, the layers of isolation. To offset this we are subjected to farts, sounds of pissing into pots, whistling, more fog horn, and other forms of isolation. Soon we find our first classic distancing device, as Winslow discovers a small votive statuette, a mermaid sculpture, like many of the sea-born relics in a Cthulhu Mythos tale. Of course, he keeps (covets) this infernal figurine, setting him on the path of his predecessor.

The dread is piled on again in the first dinner scene with Wake and Winslow. The framing of these two at their meal suggests the opening shot of the island, their table alone with the oil lamp standing out like a lighthouse beacon. Here we learn the backstory of the previous second keeper who went insane, believing in "sirens" and "merfolk," and thinking the lighthouse was enchanted by St. Elmo (all of course excellent foreshadowing). And that it is bad luck to kill a seagull, and finally the power of authority that haunted places venerate on their guests as Wake raises his toast, further setting mood and atmosphere:

> Should pale death with tremble dread
> Make the ocean caves our bed
> God who hears the surges roll
> Does to save our suppliant souls

Wake then adds, "To the next four weeks." There are other great lines of dialogue that start the conflict between these two characters and what they represent. "When the fog clears . . ." "I tend the light." "The light is mine!" These are further allusions to the contest of wills and the symbolic/allegorical nature of these characters and the story. Is Wake the "light-keeper" God, Lucifer (the "light-bringer"), or Prometheus (the "light-bringer," a.k.a. stealer of light).

Camera movement and action also swirl and entwine the narrative's movement. The camera advances in slow crawl up the spiral lighthouse stair, chains rattle beside us, the clacking of the machinery gears, to the mesmerizing blinding eye of light. Then we follow Winslow on a stroll at night on the beach, the dark water, weird vibrations, and a mermaid calling out in surreal dread. When Winslow cleans the cistern adding in a chemical mix, the result is a spiral cluster like stars in the Milky Way or one slowing losing a grasp on sanity.

Wake increases his dominant role over Winslow, referring to the light as "she." Winslow toils at his chores like Job, the light is locked and forbidden, he can see it but never touch it, on and on and on. Wake increasingly takes on a role similar to the mariner in Coleridge's *The Rime of the Ancient Mariner,* and this literary allusion becomes a motive. "Doldrum's eviler than the devil," Wake remarks. Yet as the film continues it seems to be that salvation (as symbolized in the light) makes us mad.

Literary and mythological allusion is the fuel of this lighthouse. A seagull begins to chip away at Winslow's resolve. When he falls from a scaffold while painting the lighthouse, the seagull lands and pecks at his leg. Later at night, the bird appears, tapping at Winslow's window like Poe's raven; near the sill an extinguished candle stands like the lighthouse with the orb gone out. (This might be homage to to Poe, as Eggers's first film was an adaptation of "The Tell-Tale Heart.") The film begins to blend up its literary references with myth accounting for its weirdness in a symphony of strange sequences.

Masturbation to a mermaid while cello strings mimic mating whales and the strangeness of the sea. The contest of wills becomes one of order and routine. Rain and weather dampen the mood, isolating us in with elemental dread, more toil, swabbing the floors, carting coal through a rocky crag. Wake takes on further symbolism, Odin, Zeus, Poseidon. Claims the place as "this damned rock." Claims the light as "his wife." Tell us that gulls are "the souls of sailors that met their maker." All the while the sea, the primordial salt from which we emerged, churns around the isolated isle. At night the lighthouse orb spins, casting its ray outward. It could be the eye of Sauron, searching, or the blue eye of the unfortunate victim of the narrator of Poe's "Tell-Tale Heart" penetrating Winslow's soul with its gaze. Winslow, withstanding his condition no more, kills the seagull. In an action paralleling the mariner's murder of the albatross in Coleridge's immortal poem, a curse is set, then a storm comes, and our protagonists miss their ship home, stranding them on the island. At this point, in true weird art, all natural law, including our perceptions of what and where this story is going, has been violated. But with agency of mood and atmosphere this doesn't matter. We are hooked until the end.

The "Lovecraftian" element that must be mentioned is what most people mistakenly take to be Lovecraftian—the tentacle. Sometimes a tentacle is a tentacle and sometimes it isn't. While *The Lighthouse* reveals layers of Lovecraft's influence, mostly in mood, atmosphere, and how this story is told, it is not the tentacle or anything related to those type of immemorial seahorrors; this horror is the nature of the sea itself (filling in as a metaphor for the limitless universe) and our quest for knowledge (light) and salvation. It is Lovecraftian cosmicism meets Plato's allegory of the cave, where the pain of illumination is annihilation.

The Lighthouse culminates with Wake revealing a transformation into a tentacled creature inside the inner chamber of the orb's light. He is "the keeper of secrets," knowledge is "working the lamp." Wake calls it "mine" with the same emphasis Gollum had for the ring of power. Winslow desires it, too. In his dreams he unites with a siren. They are stranded, at the mercy of the sea. They yell to each other, "What? What? What?" Wake unleashes a thundering curse: "Hark, Triton. The Sea King's Curse. The infinite waters of the dread king!" If the sea is the cosmos, we might see him as the voice of Azathoth across infinity or Cthulhu's call from the bottomless ocean depths.

The two continue on, drinking, their drunken revelry echoing somewhat *The Battle of the Lapiths and Centaurs,* as the classical allusions continue to unravel. Winslow discovers that Wake had killed the last second light-keeper, as Wake discovers Winslow killed the seagull, their contest of wills mount, Winslow attempts to vacate the island, Wake attacks him with an axe (a slight nod perhaps to Kubrick's *The Shining*—an isolation masterpiece), and in a turn of events, Winslow ends Wake's life, allowing him free access to the light. In the climactic moment, Winslow ascends to the light, his dirt- and blood-ridden face rinsed of corruption, but we see that the shear light of illumination drives him into a wailing siren screaming in acknowledgment (this is another nod to Kubrick, recalling Dave Bowman's expression when traveling through the star-gate in *2001: A Space Odyssey*). Then we behold Winslow naked and strewn over a rocky crag as seagulls pluck at his flesh, just as the vulture plucked at Prometheus' rib—for stealing fire (light) and gifting it to humanity.

The Lighthouse is packed with mythological and philosophical concepts that are set adrift in our immersive journey in this cinema of isolation. To some this is far from satisfying, as is the common reaction to any work that is not human- or human-evolution-centered, but cosmic-centered. Yet, cinematically, *The Lighthouse* is as clear a depiction of the weird as any literary transmission of mood and atmosphere can be. It is, in one tentacle, a tempest of anthropomorphic marine porn, part landscape horror, part isolation horror, and casts the iconic lighthouse as an unforgettable sinister Patronus. It is also, in another tentacle, a poetic nightmare of the sea and its call as captured in the brine's most symbolic creature, the siren. Sirens are seductive and dangerous. In Homer's *Odyssey,* Odysseus ties himself to his ship's mast and his sailors put wax in their ears so they won't be driven mad by the Siren's enchanting songs. Eggers pulls the wax out of our ears in the odyssey of *The Lighthouse,* a timeless quest for salvation and journey into madness.

About the Contributors

Michael Abolafia is a co-editor of *Dead Reckonings*.

Leigh Blackmore is an Australian horror writer, critic, editor, occultist, and musician. He was the Australian representative for the Horror Writers of America and served as the second president of the Australian Horror Writers Association.

Ramsey Campbell is an English horror fiction writer, editor, and critic who has been writing for well over fifty years. He is frequently cited as one of the leading writers in the field. His website is www.ramseycampbell.com.

Jason Ray Carney is a lecturer in the Department of English of Christopher Newport University in Newport News, Virginia. He is the co-editor of the academic journal *The Dark Man: Journal of Robert E. Howard and Pulp Studies* and the area chair of the "Pulp Studies" section of the Popular Culture Association.

Greg Gbur is a professor of physics and optical science at UNCC Charlotte. For more than a decade he has written a blog called *Skulls in the Stars* (skullsinthestars.com) about physics, horror fiction, and curious intersections between them. He has written a number of introductions to classic reprinted horror novels for Valancourt Books.

Edward Guimont recently received his Ph.D. from the University of Connecticut Department of History.

Alex Houstoun is a co-editor of *Dead Reckonings*.

Karen Joan Kohoutek, an independent scholar and poet, has published about weird fiction in various journals and literary websites. Recent and upcoming publications have been on subjects including the Gamera films, the Robert E. Howard/H. P. Lovecraft correspondence, folk magic in the novels of Ishmael Reed, and the proto-Gothic writer Charles Brockden Brown. She lives in Fargo, North Dakota.

Michael D. Miller is an adjunct professor and NEH medievalist summer scholar with numerous one-act play productions, awards, including several optioned screenplays to his credit. He has written the *Realms of Fantasy RPG* for Mythopoeia Games Publications. His poetry has appeared *Spectral Realms* and scholarly publications in *Lovecraft Annual*.

Daniel Pietersen is a writer of weird fiction and horror philosophy. He has a blog of fragmentary work and other thoughts at constantuniversity.wordpress.com.

June Pulliam teaches courses on horror fiction at Louisiana State University. She is the author of *Monstrous Bodies: Feminine Power in Young Adult Horror Fiction,* as well as many articles on fantastic young adult fiction, Roald Dahl, and zombie studies.

Daniel Raskin lives in Minneapolis, where he performs noise electronics as *permanent waves* and aggravated anti-sociality as one-half of the electro band *intercourse*.

Géza A. G. Reilly is a writer and critic with an interest in twentieth-century American genre literature. A Canadian expatriate, he now lives in the wilds of Florida with his wife, Andrea, and their cat, Mim.

Darrell Schweitzer is an American writer, editor, and critic in the field of speculative fiction. Much of his focus has been on dark fantasy and horror, although he does also work in science fiction and fantasy.

Joe Shea (The joey Zone) is an artist and illustrator. Samples of his work can be found at www.joeyzoneillustration.com.

Jerome Winter, Ph.D., is a full-time lecturer at the University of California, Riverside. His first book, *Science Fiction, New Space Opera, and Neoliberal Globalism,* was published by the University of Wales Press as part of its New Dimensions in Science Fiction series. His second book, *Citizen Science Fiction,* will be published in 2021.

Lightning Source UK Ltd.
Milton Keynes UK
UKHW021500210222
399002UK00010B/2636

9 781614 983170